The Doctor's Gift

Fiona McArthur

Chapter 1

Fergus

Fergus McVicker's twitching fingers stilled at the sight of the red-headed woman. All pre-boarding nerves forgotten. Their eyes met briefly, catching in the moment and her lips kinked delightfully before walking on.

The world slowed, she moved, and his gaze followed. Oh, dear deity! He did not have sufficient space for lust at first sight in his crowded life and that was apart from his irrational fear of flying.

Fergus dragged his eyes away from the goddess, her divine legs, heavenly red hair and a smile that glowed like the rising of the sun. The primitive and unexpected *whoomf* of desire slapped him like some navigation-deficient angel had hit his chest. He concentrated down at the research papers he was using to distract himself from the sight of the planes on the runway and tried not to lift his head.

'Dr Ailee Green?' The disembodied voice of the British flight attendant broke into the hubbub of voices. *'Would you please report to the service desk in the departure lounge.'*

Fergus gave up, checked her position. The woman, yep, *that* woman, gathered her bag and coat and glided to the desk. Another thump to his chest. Lordy, so gloriously tall, he'd always had a thing for Amazonian women. She looked supremely relaxed, unlike him.

His stomach clenched but this time not because he had to trust his life to the aircraft waiting outside the window but because Dr Ailee Green's magnetism distracted him completely as she sashayed calmly towards the uniformed attendant and presented her boarding pass for identification.

So... she was a doctor? Of something. And on his home-bound flight heading first to Singapore. Maybe all the way to Sydney if he was lucky. If she was a surgeon like him the world would indeed be small.

She wasn't classically beautiful, but something about her narrow face and widely spaced eyes resonated deeply, and the way she moved left Fergus breathless.

He shifted position so he could see her expression. Big smile, gorgeous full lips, and not afraid to look people in the eye and engage. There was something wholesome and caring about Ailee Green that slid under the barbed-wire perimeter fence he'd kept locked around his heart since Stella's death.

The colours she'd chosen to travel in were striking among the fashionable black of the Londoners — maybe that helped. Her sleeveless emerald shirt outlined her femininity as much as the soft, rusty orange trousers emphasised her height and slimness.

Dr Green made him think of sitting under trees in Sydney's Botanical Gardens on an autumn day, lunch on the pier near Luna Park, rides on the ferry across to Manly.

She was a far cry from the last fortnight at St Edna's grey facade, trying to find the key to promotion of organ donation for Australia. To be able to change the lives of people trapped by their failed organs had been enough to push through his flight phobia, leaving his daughter and work commitments, to come here.

Yes, flying over here had been important, had to be to get him on a plane and away from his daughter while things were so unsettled. St

Edna's Hospital had the highest rate of organ donation in the world and the invitation and his passion had brought him the opportunity to unlock that potential at home.

Fergus blew out a breath. The vision had quietened his nerves for a few moments at least and he wondered if he'd catch a glimpse of her again. One thing about travelling up the pointy end, the expected privacy meant he couldn't follow up on the crazy urge to wander over and chat her up!

The announcement to board tightened his nerves and he turned away.

Chapter 2

Ailee

Ailee Green followed the flight attendant, still wide-eyed at the upgrade from Economy to Business in the first leg, especially as the day had begun stressfully with the hysterical mother on the train back from her secondment in Scotland.

It turned out that the choking baby she'd helped to airway clear earlier had been the daughter of a senior airline pilot. He'd made a few calls and asked for her upgrade.

The flight attendant gestured to the seat next to the sexy guy from the departure lounge. Ailee stifled a discreet gulp. Unexpected, but nice bonus.

They exchanged surprised glances and Ailee conceded he'd been aware of her, too. Ha. She'd thought he'd watched her out there in the departure lounge, and as she settled into the big seat she fancied that despite the huge armrest that separated them, the air between their seats had begun to vibrate like the twin jet engines outside.

She tried not to blush, but the darn heat raced up her cheeks on its own agenda. She could, however, resist the urge to fan her face. 'Do I know you?' Her voice came out softer and more self-conscious than she'd intended.

'I don't think so.' He smiled at her. 'I'd remember.'

He held out his hand. With only a slight hesitation she took his fingers and the quick touch sizzled between them. Both let go at the same instant.

'I'm Fergus.' The gravelly tones in his voice, apparently invisibly attached to her nerve endings, raised the hairs on her arms and tightened her throat. Good grief.

His presence, bare centimetres away, seemed to rock her usually serene world and she had no idea why she was suddenly so susceptible to a stranger.

His full lips tilted, wicked and enticing, as if sharing the joke that they'd ended up seated together, and Ailee melted into the seat like a candle under the sun. This guy was way too good-looking and probably knew it. There was that air of command and decision about him that sat like his fitted shirt so smoothly over him.

Her neighbour had those deep, dark, bottomless black eyes she'd read about but had never believed existed... He had the lot. She glanced down at his Italian shoes near her feet. She already knew his legs were longer and stronger than hers.

Gorgeous. Terrible timing. And next to her.

Double, triple, darn.

Could he have been the one? She'd waited for years, always hoping for the flash of recognition when she'd found that spark. It may have been a leap of faith that she'd one day encounter her true soul mate, but the concept kept her from rushing into anything long term because she believed in synchronicity.

She wanted what her parents had had.

Though, if what she was feeling now was 'it', then the timing sucked. Complications she did not need right now or for the next few months because she'd be no shape for any type of dalliance.

There was always the mile-high club — sex in the clouds — while she was well enough to do it. Ailee swallowed a bubble of semi-hysterical laughter. Her wicked thought matched his black, bedroom eyes and not her common sense, and Ailee blushed again.

She'd never had a promiscuous episode in her life and she'd bet this guy had had plenty. Face it, she told herself, it was unlikely her flirty-looking seat companion was on the lookout for a meaningful relationship if he smiled like this every time a woman sat next to him.

She moistened dry lips and incredibly his eyes darkened even more. Lord, she was in a pickle, and she hoped he wasn't thinking she was flirting back. She glanced around for the flight attendant to save her.

An angel appeared with a tray of drinks. 'Champagne? Is everything all right, Dr Green?'

Ailee already knew the plane was full and she'd have to stay next to this gorgeous guy and sweat it out at least 'till Singapore. 'May I have an iced soda water, please?' To put out the fire.

The pretty flight attendant smiled, as if Ailee were the most important person in the world, until her eyes widened at the profile staring out the window next to her. Seemed her seat-companion had found something other than her that caught his attention.

The woman's gaze flitted back to Ailee.

'Not fair, is it?' Ailee said softly, and the flight attendant met her look as she handed the drink across. Both women smiled in perfect understanding.

The drink fizzed frosty as it slid down her throat and when she'd finished it the hostess returned and cleared all the glasses for take-off.

Ailee relaxed back in the seat and closed her eyes. She'd just pretend he wasn't there until she was used to him, but her heart was thumping and her brain chanted. It's him. It's him. Finally. She couldn't help the smile.

The engines roared. The runway streamed past the window and she tried not to look at him while she watched the rushing earth through half-closed lids.

The aircraft left the ground and at that moment he said, 'Sorry. Just need to talk for a minute. Are you from Sydney?' His voice sounded tight. Odd. Different from before.

She opened her eyes. His magnificent chest rose and fell quickly.

She studied him more closely as she answered. 'Coogee. In Sydney.'

She didn't ask about his origins as the aircraft creaked and bumped. He winced as clouds streamed past his window, testament to how high they were off the ground already, but he told her anyway. 'I'm from Clovelly.' Rapidly. Still stiff in the shoulders. His hand tight on his seat belt buckle. 'Not that far from Coogee. As the crow flies.' Fast quick sentences.

She sat up straighter and stopped fighting the lure of chatting with him, intrigued by his odd behaviour, a sudden urge to comfort making her want to touch his shoulder.

Instead, she said, 'I'm sorry. I should have introduced myself. I'm Ailee.' She held out her hand again and then remembered the spark before, but before she could pull back he curled his grip around hers. Like a lifeline. And hung on.

His long, elegant fingers were dry, but his upper lip held a sheen of sweat and it seemed he couldn't help a quick squeeze of her hand. 'I don't usually harass women, but I wondered if you would mind talking just for a few more minutes.' His smile seemed forced. 'Embarrassing as it is,' he mocked himself, 'I hate flying and I'm terrified of that moment after take-off. Before things even out.'

It was the last thing Ailee had expected to hear but made perfect sense. He hadn't looked like he was terrified of anything up until this moment. In fact, she would have bet he'd do a great stand-in for Tarzan wrestling a couple of lions. Not so now. She eased her fingers out of his death grip and slid her fingers around his wrist.

His pulse raced well over a hundred and she suspected at rest he'd be a fit sixty beats a minute at most.

She looked at him properly.

Clinically.

There was that faint sheen of sweat on his upper lip and a tiny flickering tic under his left eye. Shoulders and thigh muscles bunched and tense. Just as the thought triggered her professional interest they hit a patch of turbulence and his face paled to alabaster. She squeezed his wrist in sympathy and then let his arm go as he reached for the armrests.

'Sure,' she said easily. 'Flying's really not that bad, you know. The view is breathtaking.'

He looked worse at the thought and she chuckled.

He shook his head. 'Nice laugh. That makes me feel better than the story. Let's talk about something else. What's your discipline? I heard them call you Dr Green.'

'Surgery,' she obliged. She steered the conversation away from flying. 'I'm looking forward to the stop over. Have you been to Singapore before?'

The plane dipped and righted itself. He clutched the armrests until his fingers turned white and she slid her hand across his rigid forearm and down over the top of his hand to comfort him. She saw him breathe out consciously, like a woman in labour reassured by a midwife, and she squeezed his fingers where they gripped.

There was a pause when he didn't answer. The turbulence settled. He blew out a forced breath. 'Singapore? On the way over. To break the flight.' He spoke slowly, as if enunciation was a problem. Or he was going to throw up.

Poor guy. Ailee cast round in her mind for distracting conversation. She thought of the grand hotel left over from the colonial occupation of the English. 'Did you go to Raffles, the big hotel?'

He shook his head. 'I didn't leave my room.'

Rain rattled against the aircraft window but she ignored it. 'You must visit. Raffles *is* tradition. I'm told you should at least drop in and have a gin sling and crack some peanuts.'

'Peanuts?' His hand had loosened to tight, as opposed to death-grip beneath hers.

'Live a little?' Ailee wondered who she was saying that to. Him or her? 'You could always go the whole way and book for high tea. Though I tried to book from London but reservations need three days before you can get in.'

She smiled up at him and Fergus looked both stunned and delighted as if she'd just given him an unexpected gift. 'What?'

'You have a beautiful smile,' he said.

You have a beautiful everything, she thought, but she didn't say it. Just smiled again and they both settled back. She left her hand loosely clasped over his wrist.

Chapter 3

Fergus

Fergus knew the moment the plane levelled and the 'Fasten Seat Belt' sign binged and went out. Perhaps she'd leave her hand over his and he'd stay connected to her aura of calm. The stupid, embarrassing fear had seeped away with warmth of her hand over his and Fergus had the ridiculous sensation his phobia wouldn't be as big a problem ever again.

All he'd have to do was imagine Ailee Green's hand on his wrist and he'd be at peace.

She removed her fingers, leant back in her seat and closed her eyes. So much for that wish. Good to know he wasn't irresistible, despite years of avoiding the winks and nods sent his way. He never had felt he fit in the body and the face he'd been given, often wishing he'd been nondescript and ordinary, so Ailee's lack of fuss felt a nice change.

The hard part was over.

The plane hadn't crashed. He hadn't run. Or thrown up.

He could just relax through the rest of the flight until they landed and he had to take off again.

The end of that thought had a convoluted tail, like a Singapore dragon, and he shied away from it. He didn't want it to end. Right now, it felt as if his fingers wanted to be with hers for the rest of the night, maybe even for more. A crazy thought but still, he wondered how he could get her hand back.

'Dr Green.' The flight attendant murmured with a hint of urgency and an attempt not to disturb others. She startled them both. Ailee turned. Fergus frowned.

'We have an elderly gentleman in the other cabin. He appears very unwell. Can you come?'

Ailee unbuckled her seat belt immediately. 'Of course.'

Fergus undid his own belt and started to rise but the hostess gestured him back. 'Please stay seated, sir. I'll come back if Dr Green is in need of assistance.'

He subsided but added to Ailee. 'If you need help, let me know. I'm a surgeon too, but I can help.'

Ailee, which was how he thought of her now, bestowed another slightly distracted smile and thanked him before she moved off with the flight attendant.

He pulled up his video screen, stuck twiddling his thumbs, and flicked through the channels until his attention was caught with sick fascination to the flight statistics.

Wonderful.

Now he knew they were thirty-seven thousand feet above sea level and travelling at six hundred and fifty miles an hour. If a window blew out they would all freeze because it was minus sixty-five degrees outside.

Two minutes later the flight attendant was back.

'Dr Green asked if you could assist, Mr McVicker. We wish to move the man into the exit space for privacy.'

Fergus arrived in time to see the patient, an elderly man in a blue-collared shirt, roll his eyes back, clutch his chest and stop breathing. 'Cardiac arrest. I thought you might do that,' he heard Ailee mutter, and Fergus quickly scooped the frail man into the exit space, the flight attendant swished curtain shut behind them, and there was more room and privacy to work.

He looked at Ailee who had instantly re-positioned the man's airway as he was put down. Right, then. This was it with a vengeance. Time for a med school refresher.

He knelt down and loosened the collar around the man's neck and began cardiac compressions.

The flight attendant produced a resuscitation bag and oxygen cylinder while Ailee tilted his chin and fitted the mask over the gentleman's nose and mouth and inflated the man's lungs twice with rhythmic inflations of the bag.

Surprisingly, considering how long it had been since he'd involved himself in an acute, non-surgical situation, Fergus remembered earlier days and the basic life support protocols, which was all they had, came back to him.

The resuscitation continued smoothly, largely because Ailee was so quietly efficient and Fergus understood her minimal instructions perfectly. Fergus counted softly out loud and they synchronised at 30 and one for the next two breaths. There was no response from their patient. 'What about drugs and defibrillation?' Fergus asked quietly.

'Coming.' Ailee watched the man's chest closely, to ensure his lungs inflated as thirty came around again, and she didn't move her head as she spoke. 'They have a defibrillator, and emergency drugs in a sealed kit that can only be opened by a doctor. They're both on their way.'

The defibrillator arrived, and the flight attendant took over the lung inflation while Ailee positioned the defibrillator pads and gave instructions when they were to stop. Clear. And start again. After two arching pulses of electric shock through the sticky pads on the man's chest his cardiac pattern settled into a steady if weak rhythm and Ailee broke open the drug box.

A few minutes later they both sat back and watched the man as his breathing settled and his colour improved.

'Well done, Doctor.' Fergus spoke quietly. Ailee looked up and she gave him such a crooked grin he wanted to kiss her.

'Bet that made you forget you were flying.'

'I'd already forgotten.' Their eyes met and Ailee blushed. Oh yes. She looked gorgeous when she did that.

'How long until landing?' Fergus looked up at the senior steward.

'The captain said we'll be on the ground in fifteen minutes. We've diverted to Paris and an ambulance will meet us.'

An hour later, when the plane took off again for Singapore, Fergus barely noticed the ascent because of the woman next to him. He wished he was as fresh and bright as Ailee and not an emotional husk. Knew he couldn't get involved with this woman because it wasn't fair on her. There wasn't enough depth left in him to offer any woman. Yet he was touched as he watched her face while she talked about the distressed wife of the older gentleman, how she wished someone could have stayed with her in the strange country while her husband was so sick. A normal man would know how to comfort Ailee's distress without feeling awkward.

Ailee Green could brighten any life, so wonderful and genuine, and she deserved the best. Which wasn't him by a long shot. Besides, he doubted he could trust fate enough to love another woman again, or expose himself to that type of loss for a second time.

And his daughter deserved any reserves of attention he had left.

Trouble being, Ailee was captivating. And engaging as if he interested her. She waved her long fingers in the air as she kept the conversation rolling. 'I always wondered if defibrillation would cause the cabin lights to flicker.'

Fergus thought about that. 'Obviously not. That probably means the navigation equipment is still working, too.'

She watched him with sudden intensity and raised her brows, 'I told you flying was safe.' But she was smiling.

Neither of them felt like sitting quietly now. She'd travelled widely and had anecdotes from almost every continent, and she followed his lead and never once mentioned her role in medicine.

Fergus was careful to keep the topics general, protecting them both from silliness. Had told himself if he didn't know where she practised, he wouldn't search for her. But, but he still found out that she lived with her younger brother and mother in a huge rambling house near Coogee beach, drove a thirty-year-old Mercedes that used to belong to her father, and loved heavy metal rock as well as vintage country music.

Dinner came and went and they discussed how both had a parent who'd emigrated from Scotland, discussed cosmopolitan London and the sheer age of the Roman ruins in the Tower Of London, which surprisingly they'd both visited on this trip, though hers had been a working holiday in Scotland most of the time.

Other times they kept their own thoughts and he found her incredibly restful in the silences.

Eventually the cabin lights dimmed and everyone settled to rest for the few hours before breakfast, but despite the comfort of his sleeping pod Fergus found he couldn't sleep. Ailee stirred emotions that had lain dormant since Stella had died. He wouldn't cope if he fell in love with another woman. Nor would his daughter. He knew that. Couldn't risk the already difficult relationship they had. But he wished.

He could feel his world rocking, like stormy weather, worse than turbulence in flight, and he needed to be careful. But at least he was feeling something. It had been so long since he'd actually suffered emotion since Stella died. It would be so easy and so dangerous to fall for this woman. To ask to spend more time with her — even just in Singapore.

A moment in time, just twenty-four hours of a dream, time out from the real world with Ailee, and to recharge his faith in the good times that were out there, as long as they both obeyed the rules.

His mouth compressed. As long as he obeyed the rules! Except - who knew the rules?

The plane flew on and breakfast arrived as the blinds were raised. A pale sunrise pinked the sky outside the windows and a few minutes later Ailee began to stir beside him.

'Good morning.' He wanted to add, *sleepyhead*, but that was too familiar for strangers. But he smiled at her tousled hair and sleep creased cheek. This was how she looked in the mornings — good enough to eat.

The thought stoked the fire in his belly that had simmered all night and he had to look away because if he didn't he'd lean over and kiss her properly awake. And that would get him locked up and taken off the plane by police when they landed.

When she'd had time to wake properly and had her first cup of tea, he asked the question he'd deliberated on all night. 'If I secure a reservation today, will you share high tea at Raffles with me?'

Her eyes widened, and pink dusted the high cheek bones of her face. He forced himself not to hold his breath.

She hesitated. 'I doubt you'd get one before we fly on to Sydney.'

He shrugged. 'Let me see what I can do while you at least think about it. Which hotel are you staying at?' He opened his laptop and logged on.

He thought he detected some reluctance in divulging the information and reminded himself that she had every right to be wary of him. 'The Singapore Dragon,' she supplied.

Delight warmed him at her answer. As he was. There was that Karmic tail again. 'Serendipity.' He smiled at this good luck and though she didn't meet his eyes she smiled too.

'What a coincidence.'

'I'll let you know when they get back to me, then.'

Chapter 4

Ailee

What was she doing?

Ailee argued with herself as she dragged her overnight case past the empty luggage carousel where crowds waited for their bags to appear. She'd learnt long ago it was better to pack a few interchangeable clothes and avoid the whole extra luggage hassle.

Fergus McVicker just wanted a fling.

She'd been trained long ago not to talk to strangers – especially heart-tugging scared-of-flying ones – but apart from the medical emergency, it had been fun.

Customs cleared quickly and she spotted her name on the hire-car driver's board as she went through the automatic doors. 'Dr Green?'

'That's right.' She handed over her case and followed the shorter man out to his Lexus. The Singapore heat hit like an oven door open and she revelled in it after the cold of Britain. She should be resting and writing up her review of her Scottish secondment for the hospital board while she was here, not gallivanting around with the hunky Mr McVicker. Despite ringing her possible soulmate bells, he also had bad timing signs written all over him.

Ailee barely saw the glorious red and purple bougainvillea lining the road from airport to the city. During their conversations she'd become glaringly aware that Fergus had avoided any mention of Sydney, their work, or meeting up when they got home. That at least was a good thing for the next three months.

But now there was this afternoon tea thing.

At Raffles.

Something she'd always wanted to do.

If she agreed to meet him today, well, afternoon tea could lead to drinks, and drinks to dinner, and dinner to goodness knew what!

She needed to highlight his lack of interest in their mutual vocation and accept he was ensuring there was no 'ever after' planned for the two of them… just a Singapore fling. She shouldn't want that. Did she?

Trouble was, she was way out of her depth. As an old-fashioned girl, she didn't do flings. Even Singapore ones.

Despite this, Ailee couldn't believe how tempted she was.

They'd connected, she guessed. Yes, Fergus had bedroom eyes, but they were kind eyes with understanding, and recognition, so beautiful it was downright hard to look away from him. Add the play of muscles from well-defined arms, powerful yet elegant hands, and strength and agility in a body to sigh over. Well, all of him was hard to look away from. Even in the midst of the crisis on the plane, a part of her had been impressed when he'd carried that man to the galley as if he were as light as a doll, and then deferred easily to her more current expertise.

The flight phobia he'd admitted to only made him more intriguing because it called to the nurturing part of her that she'd only had the opportunity to practise on her patients or her brother. She felt for him in his distress.

What was it that activated a subliminal connection between them? Whatever it was she was sure he felt it, too. She couldn't remember when she'd last worked in an emergency as easily as she had with Fergus during the resuscitation of that poor man on the flight.

And later, they'd talked. About everything not personal, and she still didn't know how he had so adroitly skirted sharing such information. He'd prompted her on places she'd visited – places he'd never been to – and she'd only half-explain then see he understood what she'd described perfectly. She could visualise as clearly when he described something. As if he sent the picture to her mind so clearly.

Other times during the flight they'd sat in silence and felt no need to fill the gaps. She'd never had that with a man. Was it all just a ships-in-the-night attraction that she'd regret following or not following?

She shivered and the driver caught her eye in the mirror.

'Air-conditioner too cold, Doctor?'

Ailee felt the warmth in her cheeks. Damn. Just thinking about Fergus had her blushing, and cursing, more than she had since her teens. 'No, thank you. I'm fine.'

She stared out the window at building construction as they came closer to the city.

So? What was she going to do?

The sensible thing would be to tell Fergus she had a review to write and stay safe in her room. That a future with this man was not a high percentage. The downside being she could miss out on an incredible day in her study-filled life.

But what if this was her one time to cross this man's path? What if this was the real thing and she'd been too timid to risk exploring the possibility? Then he would disappear when they landed at Sydney Airport and she would then spend the rest of her life searching for someone to match him?

Damn.

Again.

If he was her perfect match, his timing was atrocious.

The next three months weren't going to be much fun for her, although she didn't for one second regret her coming operation. She just wished she'd met Fergus at a different time in her life.

Check-in at the hotel passed in a blur of passports, credit cards and declining help with her luggage, while she wrestled with her social dilemma. Clarity came as the plastic key was encased in its embossed cardboard folder.

'Enjoy your stay, Dr Green.'

She needed to be sensible. 'Can I leave a message for another guest, please?'

Ten minutes later the force of the water on her shoulders felt wonderful after the gentle spray of the showers she'd experienced in Britain, and she forced herself to slow breaths and deep sighs.

This was more sensible.

She'd decided not to meet Fergus. Would finish her report then go for a walk. Excellent. She flipped open her case and pulled out her computer, found the page. Glanced at the clock digits as they changed. Tried not to watch the morning traffic increase outside her window.

She wanted to be out there.

Walking off the agitation.

Not thinking about Fergus.

The doorbell rang and she quietened the flutter of nerves the sound ignited. 'This is too good a hotel to give him my room number,' she said out loud to calm the thudding in her chest as she moved towards the door.

The bellboy held up an exquisite basket of delicate Singapore orchids. A note nestled among the perfect blooms.

'Dr Green?' the boy checked.

'Yes, that's me.' She took the basket from him and sighed. She resisted the urge to tip, having read hotels in Singapore discouraged tipping. 'Thank you.'

The boy beamed and turned away.

Ailee closed the door and carried the basket across to the table under the window.

'Thank you for your hand and your delightful company on the flight from London. My room number is 2001. High tea is at three, I'll be there anyway. F.'

This hotel stood only twenty stories high, which meant he was at the top. Typical. He'd been in Business Class after all. The flowers nodded, regal and perfectly beautiful, as she adjusted their position on the desk. It was only ten o'clock in the morning.

Ailee dialled his room number and he picked it up on the first ring. 'The flowers are lovely, thank you.'

'I'm glad you like them. I wasn't trying to change your mind.'

'Sure you were,' she drawled, and she heard him chuckle. 'Lucky for you I need to get out. Would you like me to show you Singapore this morning and I'll think about afternoon tea?'

'Yes, please.'

She smiled into the phone at his simple answer.

When she met him downstairs she felt the warmth of his appraisal, and the pitter-patter of her heart said she appreciated him too. Okay. She was glad she'd agreed to come.

Heads turned as they walked across the foyer, a very tall woman and an even taller, commanding man, and Ailee felt a little like a groupie accompanying a rock star. He held her arm, gently but firmly, and the skin under his fingers tingled as he showed her to the limousine he'd hired.

He ushered her into the vehicle and as he climbed in after her, she inhaled his freshly showered scent and the divine masculine aftershave as she did up her seat belt. What was she doing?

Foreign country. Unknown man. Driving away with him.

But he was a surgeon like her. Had a reputation to safeguard, as did she.

They rode across to Sentosa on the skyway and she noticed the slightest of hesitations, only because she's become so keenly attuned to his body language.

He didn't complain when she recommended they take the elevator to the top of the giant stone lion's head, the Merlion.

From the platform Ailee gazed out over the lush greenery and away to the water and across the bay before recalling her self-appointed tour-guide status and pointing out landmarks. They discussed the British influence on Singapore and the fabulous growth of the new city. Talking to Fergus was so easy, so comfortable, no matter what the topic.

Fergus, with laughter in his eyes, bought her a snowball with a miniature skyway as a memento. Because it was inexpensive, she let him. The flowers back in her hotel room probably cost him an arm and a leg and she would not have accepted another pricey gift.

On the way back they stopped at the Skyroom, which lay between the two ends of the aerial road over the lush greenery. They drank champagne at the edge of the open-air restaurant overlooking the unbroken view so high above the tropical gardens below. All the while Fergus had a soft smile on his face as he watched her.

Ailee felt as if she were flying again and not all of it was to do with their height from the ground. Flying? Something about flying...

She clapped her hand to her head. 'That's why you hesitated. Taken you to so many high places and ignored your fear of heights.'

Chapter 5

Fergus

'I was amused.' Fergus shook his head and relaxed back into the lounge, thinking how beautiful she was. 'I think you've cured me. That's why I bought you the snowball. As a thank-you.'

Ailee made his heart ache, Fergus thought, as she leaned against the gold cushions in her Singapore-red sundress with her long legs bent at the knee and casually crossed at the ankle.

He struggled to keep the conversation going as his attraction spiked and desire rose. What were they discussing? That's right — his aversion to heights. 'It's the actual plane, take-off, not heights, I don't like. I'm afraid the whole motorised flight concept makes me shudder. The cable car isn't my favourite vehicle either but—' his glance brushed over her and he smiled '—strangely, I'm much calmer about it now.'

She leant towards him, her face concerned, her shampoo scent teasing him on the breeze, making him want to sink his nose into her hair and breathe. She looked at him as if he was the most fascinating person in the world. The cynical side of Fergus dreaded her finding out he was just a shell of a man.

But he didn't feel a shell when he was with her. He felt buoyed by her energy, intoxicated by her laugh, alive for the first time in two years

- and too afraid to ask why. Already he was questioning his internal debate for following up their acquaintance in Sydney.

The waiter arrived with their seafood lunch and the conversation moved away from his flight phobia as they discussed their plans for the rest of the day.

Their driver suggested the Botanical Gardens and through them the path to the orchid garden and the promise of tranquillity attracted them.

As they walked a leafy trail to a waterfall, Fergus held Ailee's hand in his and even managed to comment sensibly on native birds and several dragon lizards, despite the fact that all he could think of was the feel of her skin against his. They discussed environmental issues and wildlife protection, and after a wonderful ninety minutes of meandering among the serene gardens and trees they sat and ate tiny sandwiches and icecream before heading back to the where their driver waited. Fergus felt more at peace than he had for a long time.

When they were back in the limo, Ailee sighed back in the rear seat and turned to Fergus. 'Thank you. I loved the gardens and orchid houses. It was amazing, thank you. I don't see flowers like that often.'

'I enjoyed it, too.' Very much. 'Are you a gardener?'

'I'm more a beach person,' she supplied. 'You said you come from Clovelly. Do you walk on the beach?'

No. He didn't. Never. 'Not often. I gather you do?'

'Whenever I can.' Her face lit as she found a new enthusiasm to wax about and he shook his head. He wished he felt these things, these passions and joys, but these last two years he'd felt cold and stifled. Old and tired.

Except, it seemed, when he was with Ailee. She did not need his wet blanket on her joy for life but for the moment he would drink her in and live for today.

By the time they arrived back in the city they were ready for afternoon tea at the magnificent white-columned Raffles, beneath the rows of waving ceiling fans.

There'd been no more talk of her not joining him for the treat.

They started in the famous bar and Ailee dragged him by the hand to a table between the magnificent staircase and the window overlooking the terrace. Tropical birds chattered outside the frame and tourists laughed and cracked nuts as they sipped their umbrella'd drinks. The place vibrated with laughter and he felt out of step.

A bowl of peanuts, still in their shells, sat in the middle of their table and Fergus glanced down as his feet crunched over the discarded shells that covered the floor. 'Odd housekeeping.'

He raised his eyebrows at Ailee and she laughed.

'It's all part of the atmosphere,' she said.

A pretty waitress carried her order book over to their table. 'Gin slings?' she asked, branding them as tourists.

'Yes, please.' Ailee answered before Fergus could say anything, and she turned to him and smiled. Yes, he would have drunk dishwater if she'd asked at that moment.

'You *have to* drink a gin sling when you come here, it's part of the tradition.'

'So many traditions to agree to.' He cracked a nut and offered her the bean-shaped centre. 'And eat peanuts?'

'Absolutely.' She took the nut and lifted the shells from his palm to discard them wickedly on the floor, as others were doing.

'Decadent,' he said lazily, and savoured the way she slid the morsels into her mouth. She wasn't looking at him, distracted by the noise and sights, and her lips were full and lush and the tip of her pink tongue slipped out to lick the taste. He closed his eyes and struggled to divert his thoughts.

'So, you've been here before?' Inane, but at least he'd managed to say something.

Ailee looked back and he enjoyed the pleasure on her face. 'Once. With my parents when my dad was alive. I loved it. The bar used to be much longer but I still adore the fans that are all joined together across the ceiling.'

His question came out sooner than he'd intended. 'So, what are your plans when you get home?'

She looked away from him and disappointment clouded his euphoria. Her face changed, even in profile, closing from the openness he'd savoured, the smile slipping away, her eyes cast down. That wasn't a good sign.

'I'm tied up for a few months.' When she said that her voice seemed lower and her expression turned evasive under his intense scrutiny. 'A family thing, so I'm off work until that's finalised,' she said.

Fergus tried to regain some of the closeness he could feel slipping away. Did she miss them? Had bad news? He searched for a new connection. The taste of the peanuts tasted more like chalk on his tongue. He looked around and the room had dimmed. The gloss of the furnishings now gloomy and the chatter of the tourists gone quiet or was that the sudden mood between them.

What happened then?

His need to find rapport made him dive into speech. 'Families are important, even when things aren't so smooth on the home front. I'm not a great parent, I'm afraid. There's just myself and my daughter.'

Ailee's face whipped around, eyes wide, her mouth opening and closing in surprise, but the moment was interrupted before she could speak as the waitress arrived with their drinks.

Lucky. He needed to stop before he changed all the rules of the Singapore stopover. One that was not supposed to go anywhere beyond a day out with a woman he liked.

Friendship. New experience. This woman. He lifted his glass to her, the red coloured cocktail like Ailee in its vibrancy, the pineapple slice and the maraschino cherry ridiculous. Time to drink the medicine, and his first sip was cautious. Sweet, yet sour. Thankfully the drink wasn't as bad as he'd feared it would be.

Ailee watched him and he tried to keep his face noncommittal. 'You thought you'd hate it, didn't you?' she accused him and some of the amusement was back in her voice. He would have drunk that dishwater to make her happy again.

Fergus took another sip. 'I'm not a gin fan but this is very pleasant. What's in it?'

'Gin. Cherry Brandy. Pineapple Juice.' She ticked them off her fingers. 'Lime Juice. Cointreau. Dom Benedictine. Grenadine and a dash of Angostura Bitters.'

He smiled. 'And I can see garnished with a slice of pineapple and a cherry.' Tilted his head at her. 'How did you remember that?'

She touched her temple. 'I have a very good memory.' He laughed as she went on. 'You can only have one because they are very expensive and I'm paying.' Ailee reached out and stole the bill before he could look.

That made him smile. 'Who said you were paying?'

'I did.' Ailee raised her chin. 'You paid for the car. If I pay now I don't have to feel bad about you paying for lunch and afternoon tea.'

Not something he was used to but he could see it mattered to her. 'It's a deal. Shake on it.' He held out his hand and she hesitated before she put her hand in his. Their eyes met and he remembered the sensation as soon as they touched. He had the feeling she did too, and her warmth shot into him like a surge from a charger. Buzzing his lowered batteries. Heating and stimulating and addictive. He didn't want to let go.

They sat there for a moment and then Ailee eased her fingers out of his hold and picked up her glass. His empty fist returned to his thigh but he could still feel her warmth on his fingers.

She turned to check the clock on the wall and began to swallow her cocktail as if it wasn't famous and apparently very expensive. Studied him for a moment and there was a hint of reserve when she said, 'I think we'd better go for afternoon tea. They have a strict timetable.'

The distance was back.

Fergus finished his own drink and stood to pull out her chair. As she rose, she put down Singapore dollars on the bill and smiled at the waitress as the girl approached. 'Thank you, that was lovely and wonderful service.'

'You are most welcome.' The girl smiled and Fergus stored that away. Ailee's personal touch, the way she connected with people, made them smile, were more reasons why Ailee touched him.

When they were seated in the more formal room for afternoon tea, Ailee's natural exuberance seemed to have returned. 'I've always wanted to do this. Thank you.'

He relaxed back into the chair. 'Thank you for your company. I've enjoyed the day with you.'

Ailee grinned. 'Wait until you taste the cakes.'

Fergus looked across where another couple were choosing from the cart. He wrinkled his nose.

Her eyes met his. 'You didn't think you'd like the gin sling.'

'My daughter is the cake lover, not me.' Another unexpected share. Stop it.

'I wanted to ask.' She put her elbows on the table and rested her chin on her hands to watch him. 'Tell me about your daughter. How old is she?'

Fergus gazed out the window and in his mind's eye he saw his daughter, not the branches of the tree that brushed the side of the building. In his mind Simone glowered at him. 'Simone is twelve and very clever.' He looked up at her. 'She has an excellent memory too.'

Ailee beautiful mouth curved.

'Since her mother died, we haven't had much common ground. I think I've failed her.' He hadn't meant to say the last sentence but that's what happened when you started to let people in. Conversation became a landslide.

Ailee's eyes softened but she looked away. Well, he'd blown that by being honest. He didn't want her to think he didn't try to connect with Simone. 'I love my daughter but I work long hours. Get called away often. I've tried to be there for her but it hasn't worked that well. My wife died just before Simone turned ten. It's been hard to spend the time with my daughter that she needs.'

Her gaze returned to his and he realized he'd been mistaken. She wasn't distancing herself, just giving him time to organise his thoughts.

'So, since then you've brought your daughter up on your own?' she asked.

'Both sets of grandparents died before she was born. Martha and Douglas, my housekeeper and her husband, have been amazing. She talks to them.' Fergus knew how lucky he'd been. 'I don't know what we would have done without them.'

She stirred her tea. Could see she was taking care choosing her words. 'Why do you feel that she doesn't talk to you as much as to your staff?' Ailee chewed her lip and he appreciated she was wary of crossing boundaries.

'I don't think of them as staff. I'm sure Simone doesn't either. Martha and Douglas are more like family.'

A few women he knew weren't worried about boundaries and he'd never talked to anyone about Simone before. Maybe he should have. A woman's perspective might be the help he needed to understand.

'I hate that lost closeness with my daughter.' And despaired he'd ever regain the rapport they'd once had. 'Her mother was there one day and gone the next. My wife, Stella, died after a routine operation. A procedure of course I'd told Simone would be fine. I'm afraid the shock of her mother's death destroyed Simone's ability to trust me or my profession. After all, I'd said, "Mummy will be fine."'

He shook his head at the waste. 'We all assumed wrongly. The operation was minor but the consequences a disaster. She had a reaction to the anaesthetic and then an aneurysm.'

'I'm sorry.' Ailee put the teacup back in the saucer with infinite care before wiping her fingers carefully, deliberately with the napkin. He liked the way she took her time before rushing into gushes of sympathy.

'It would be terrible for a young girl to lose her mother at that age. It must be doubly hard for you.'

He didn't want her pity, just a suggestion of what might help him connect with his daughter. Or perhaps he should never have started this conversation. Too deep, too soon. 'Simone is in high school. I was doing such a poor job of keeping her happy I've enrolled her at a boarding school through the week until we sort it out.'

Her eyebrows went up. 'Does she like that?' Ailee sounded doubtful that any child would be impressed with that idea.

He thought about his answer. 'It's early days, but Simone is self-sufficient and likes company.'

'Or is good at pretending?' Ailee suggested.

He sighed. 'She can't be worse off than she was with me. We fought about everything.'

Ailee's lack of comment made him think she disapproved of Simone in boarding school, but she had no idea how hard it had been. The last time Simone had run from the room crying he'd vowed he'd have to find a way to make her happier.

Fergus tried to explain. 'I thought boarding school with the company of other girls might help.'

Her look said she had reservations. 'It's none of my business. It must work better for you both if you work long hours. As long as she doesn't miss your housekeeper and her husband, too?'

Relieved, Fergus nodded and ignored the way Ailee's comment had pricked his confidence about Simone's schooling.

He'd save those thoughts for later review.

They both stirred their tea. Fergus broke the silence. 'Tell me about your childhood.' He'd shared his most personal thoughts and feelings, and it's only fair to ask something of her. Plus, he wanted to know.

She smiled. 'I'm boring.'

'Feel free to bore me.' He didn't think he would ever tire of listening to her voice.

Ailee shrugged and her gaze drifted around the room. 'My parents had the best love affair. Made me a romantic.' She blushed and then hurried on. 'My dad was a fun guy and we did lots of mad things. He had his pilot's licence and an old rag and tube aeroplane that was so noisy you had to wear earmuffs to protect your ears.'

'Where did he keep an aeroplane in the city?'

Ailee smiled at the memories. 'At an aerodrome near Camden, but it's a lot busier now than it was when I was a child. We'd drive down on Sundays and have a picnic and fly a few circuits and he'd let me steer through the clouds.'

He could imagine a little girl like Ailee bouncing up and down on a seat as they'd driven to the outlying airport to have fun with her dad. He wished he had memories like that with Simone. Maybe he needed to make some happen — just not with a plane. 'It sounds great, except for the flying part.'

Ailee looked up at the humour in his voice and she grinned at him. 'But I like aeroplanes and you don't.'

'Did you do anything on the ground that was fun?'

She nodded, her eyes sparkling. Fergus savoured the way her face lit up at her memories. Not boring in the least.'Dad had a passion for boats for a while and we tried sailing.'

'Now, I can enjoy a day sailing.'

Ailee shook her head. 'We had to sell the boat because if the sea turned choppy and the boat rocked, we all got seasick and there was no one left to steer while we fell around the deck, throwing up over the side.'

'Well, thanks for the graphic detail,' Fergus teased.

'No problem.' She sat back and her eyes crinkled, and he realised how fortunate he was to be here at this minute with this woman opposite him.

Her eyes grew distant with memories and he understood she was done sharing. Her movement pulled the red material of her dress against her breasts and his mouth dried.

Fergus shifted under the sudden tsunami of desire that hit him, much bigger than the waves Ailee had just mentioned. He tore his eyes away from her and stared at the ceiling. 'This is a great room.'

Unfortunately, the colonial surroundings didn't prove as distracting as Fergus had hoped, though he didn't think any location would drown out what he suddenly wanted to do.

'Isn't it?' Ailee sighed back into the chair. 'I love this place and it's fab to be inside the formal rooms.'

Fergus needed to hold Ailee close in his arms, and maybe run his fingers down her amazing cheekbones, circle her beautiful mouth with his fingertip, before doing what he needed to do — kiss her. He had to kiss her. Taste her.

His ears buzzed with the need.

'I said, aren't you going to have any food?' Ailee's lips curved, enticing, soft and smiling at him, and he blinked and came back to the present.

The waiter stood resplendent in his uniform beside their table. Regally, the man presided over a silver-handled trolley festooned with tiny delicate cakes and slices, obviously waiting for a decision.

Fergus wasn't that kind of hungry. Not that kind of hungry at all.

'I think you need your bed,' Ailee said as she accepted a miniature butterfly cake onto her plate.

'I think I do, too.' His voice came out softer and deeper than he'd intended and there was no doubt what he meant. He watched the blush run up her cheeks.

Fergus cleared his throat. 'Sorry. You're right. I'm tired. I've gone absent-minded on you.' He chose a chocolate slice he didn't want and forced himself to swallow a bite past his dry throat.

Disapproving of their meagre selections the waiter moved on. Fergus didn't even notice.

This woman had him in a state he hadn't been since a kid on his first date. It would be amusing. If it wasn't so dangerous.

'Perhaps we could meet for dinner after a few hours' sleep,' Fergus suggested.

'I'd like that,' she said.

Chapter 6

Ailee

After a tight-lipped and awkwardly tense trip back to their hotel with growing awareness tingling her skin, Ailee was glad to be helped out of the limousine by the doorman. Even the steamy warmth outside the limo seemed cooler than the heat inside.

Things had changed since afternoon tea.

The previous ease she'd felt with Fergus was now overlaid with an awareness that both of them were trying, desperately, to hide. She'd felt it rise at the table in Raffles and shift into the tangible sexual tension that vibrated between them now. Maybe it had been the discussion of families, or the sun, or the sling, or maybe it had just grown during the time they'd spent together.

Ailee wasn't sure, but there was no denying they were very, very aware of each other. When Fergus cupped her elbow as they stood together and waited for the lift, Ailee felt the warmth of his hand as if she'd brought a bubble of the Singapore heat from outside into the air-conditioned coolness of the hotel.

The lift bell sang its chime and the golden doors opened in front of them. Her gaze was caught by the mirror at the back of the lift and the reflection of the two of them standing so close, eyes meeting in the mirror. Goosebumps lifted the hairs on her arms and her belly began a slow burn. Fergus turned and stretched one hand out to the control panel and raised his eyebrows questioningly.

'Ten,' Ailee said softly, and he pressed her floor button along with his own. Half of her sighed with relief and the other chewed her lip with indecision.

If she said something she knew he would come to her room, but she couldn't do it. She didn't know him that well. They had met barely twenty-four hours ago.

So why did she feel she knew this man on a level she'd never known any man?

Fergus squeezed her elbow and slid his hand up her arm, her neck, her cheek, and he cupped her face and turned her to him. She felt the heat slice through her.

'Thank you for your company,' he said as the lift stopped at her floor and he leaned in to kiss her goodbye.

His breath, chocolate-cake and male, followed by his mouth, firm and brushing, as his lips met hers. A soft, gentle brush that made her breath pull in. His warmth captured her as he brushed softly, teasingly again, his mouth provocative and she leaned in. Suddenly his hard chest pulled against her own softness. Mixing her breath with his in tiny nibbles, until his tongue brushed the center of her lips in a slow sweep. She gasped and her heart sped.

Her mouth opened to his, drawing him in. The lift doors closed, locking them together. The restraint they'd both held disappeared into the small space as all thoughts of leaving the cage were lost and she jammed closer. Into him. Harder.

Strong arms circled her as all the dancing around the attraction that flared between them was declared a waste of precious time, because this was where she wanted to be. His hand on her face, his other around her shoulders pressing her into him. His thighs against hers.

The lift carried them swiftly to the top floor of the building.

Ailee didn't know how they passed through the penthouse door, but obviously Fergus had found his key and inserted the card successfully, because when she opened her eyes, she was being carried across the room in his strong arms.

Ailee sank her head back against his gorgeous chest. She'd always had a weakness for muscular chests. No one had actually carried her for many years — not since she'd grazed her knees as a skinny five-year-old — and Fergus carried her as if she were still as tiny as a child.

She savoured being whisked through the rooms in this man's arms, she was flying, light as a feather and she could almost believe she was one of those petite women she'd always admired. He settled her at the edge of his bed and traced her brow with his finger as if she were the most fragile of Dresden china.

'You captured me the first time I saw you. Do you know that?' His quiet words lifted the hairs on her arms and she smiled at the way this man could make her feel more sensations and emotions than any man from her past.

Her mouth turned suddenly dry from nerves. 'When I sat next to you on the plane?' She remembered that moment. She'd thought she'd been the only one who'd been aware of attraction.

He traced her cheeks and lips and pressed a soft, fleeting kiss on her mouth before going on. 'Before that. In the terminal, across a crowded room, like in all the best movies, you shone like a golden star.'

There was nothing she could do against the power he held over her. He was kind and funny and the sweeping conversations they'd had exposed the ferocity of his intellect. She felt as if she'd found someone who understood her.

But why now? When she couldn't commit to anything beyond this moment.

But when he drew her into his arms there was no real world, nothing beyond here and now. Only Fergus to lose herself in.

He kissed her again and she was swept into a storm of sensation. The taste and feel and scent of him surrounded her. Engulfed her.

His strength and gentleness created havoc as he slipped her dress straps down her arms and exposed her body to the air-conditioned coolness in the room. The way he looked at her made her want to purr with unexpected pride and blush with her own wantonness.

Shameless, her fingers flew as she unbuttoned his shirt and slipped her hands beneath the fabric to run them over the hard planes of his chest. So hot, so hard, so perfect and masculine and sexy and here. *Hers.* She needed to feel more than his skin under her hands, she needed to feel all of him against her body. Now.

He stripped her dress lower, brushed her taut breast with his tongue before staring down at her with a fierce delight. Leaving her nipples damp. Cold. Puckering.

She felt powerful, strong and fiercely desired by this golden man above her, and she reached up and stroked his muscled neck and shoulders as he lowered his face again to kiss her mouth. Tongue hot and thrusting and ravenous for her. As if searching for secrets they could share together.

There was nothing she could do against the power he held over her.

Nothing else she wanted to do but be here.

The rights and wrongs of this craziness and knowing she couldn't follow up their encounter in Sydney were all swept aside as her body responded to the feel of him against her.

'Yes.'

The shrill sound of the room telephone finally penetrated the fog that surrounded them both.

Fergus groaned and reached with one hand to lift the phone. With the other he captured her fingers to stop her instinctive pull away.

But his caller created that distance.

'Daddy?' She heard the word.

So did Fergus of course. 'Simone! What's wrong? Why are you crying?'

Fergus let go of Ailee's hand and turned his shoulder to face away from her. His voice dropped in volume and Ailee looked away. Heard, 'What do you mean, not good?'

Cold sense splashed her alert. It wasn't just them. He'd told her about his young daughter who lost her mother.

What was she doing here? She pulled the top of her dress up and slid to the edge of the bed.

Simone didn't need her father being with another woman.

Didn't need him even falling for another woman if that was where this was going.

Let alone one who was going into surgery for an operation that was anything but minor. One with risks far greater than those that had taken Simone's mother. Ongoing risks.

She blew out a sad sigh. Shook her head. She could search him out when all this was over if she was well and he was interested.

She thought he was interested. Smiled grimly at the stupid thought. Not just sex and a Singapore Sling, but perhaps something more.

She looked around the room and reluctantly thanked Fergus's daughter for the phone call. Ailee's loyalties lay in a different direction too for the next few months and she couldn't divide herself at this point. Couldn't distract herself from what mattered.

He put the phone down and gave her a whimsical smile. 'Where were we?'

'I was about to leave.'

'Because my daughter rang?' he asked quietly, carefully, as if wanting to understand.

She gestured with her hand. 'Because this isn't the right time for this... for whatever this is between us.'

Fergus raised his eyebrows. 'What else have you got planned that makes this timing so bad?'

She nearly told him then, but what if he said that didn't matter, when she knew it did? What if he tried to talk her out of the operation — not that he could — but it would create more dilemmas that she couldn't face. She'd had enough of that from others. Better to leave the whole subject alone.

She said, 'It's a family thing.'

His face twisted into a cynical smile. 'What if this is our one chance?'

She lifted her eyes to his and acknowledged that the concept was possible, and something she too had considered, but there was nothing she could do about that. Not now. Look where it had got her. Sitting on a bed with a stranger.

She lifted her gaze to his. 'That would be sad but I can't do this now.'

He stared back. Eyes dark and a little despairing. 'I think it would be more like a tragedy. This could be the start of something special, Ailee. Do you feel that?'

She nodded but her heart told her she really should go.

He smiled. Sadly. Warm and compassionate, still sexy but not about sex and she had no idea how he'd done it. 'Let's slow the whole thing down.'

She almost laughed. But it would have come out bitter. 'I was. I'm leaving.'

His hand rose slowly – like he wanted her to take it. To trust him. Really. She'd just been half naked with his mouth on her skin.

'Please.' Softly, teasing but again not with sex. 'We could do something really radical?'

She blew out a breath. Totally off balance now. 'I think this is all radical enough.'

He chuckled. 'I was thinking how good you felt in my arms. How amazing you make me feel just by being here. And if that's the same for you, and we don't want to rush... What say we sleep? Platonic but close.'

She looked at him. His shirt open. His glorious chest making her ache to run her nails down the corrugated muscles.

Making her burn to bury her face in him. 'Yeah, like that's going to happen.'

'You slept in the plane. I know. I watched you. I've been awake all night. Seeing you. Enjoying the scenery but tired. Come back down beside me. We could both rest, even sleep. When we wake, have dinner with me.' He patted the bed. 'I'll put my shirt back on. Just lie beside me and we can talk.' Fergus smiled one last, entreating smile at her and any resistance she'd had melted like snow in Singapore. 'I could hold your hand.'

If any other man had promised her bed with no seduction she would have doubted him.

But somehow, what Fergus said, she could believe.

If she didn't make love with him, then she hadn't lied by omission or led him on too much. Had she?

'I won't sleep,' she dithered.

'Then just rest.' He patted the bed again. 'We could eat in the room later if you prefer, we don't have to change.' He waved his hand. 'It's much more fun here than in your lonely room.'

That was true and the bed was soft and the cushions indulgent. The penthouse, now she looked around, was a sumptuous suite with panoramic windows. The view city scape and distant harbour – spectacular - and that was apart from Fergus.

His hand slid into hers and she lay back down beside him. He didn't try anything, and his hand held hers warmly but with gentle pressure. Slowly she relaxed. After some desultory conversation, to her surprise, her eyes grew heavy.

Chapter 7

Ailee

Ailee woke, the room dark with block-out curtains pulled shut, and a man she'd met twenty-four hours ago asleep, breathing deeply, beside her. Their hips touched, hands loosely clasped as if they were old friends or lovers, but she was even less sure she was doing the right thing by the widower Fergus.

There may be something unknown and powerful between them, and she hoped one day she'd find out if fate, who'd sat them next to each other on that long-haul flight, decided to help again. Or even if, when she could – *if* she could – she'd try to at least ensure they met again and reconsider the possibilities.

Surely she could find him again, another surgeon in Sydney, especially one who lived near her.

She'd make that happen.

Ailee gazed at the ceiling and thought of what lay ahead of her. And what lay behind Fergus and his twelve-year-old daughter.

She hadn't forgotten, she'd just been submerged under the powerful forces of the man lying asleep beside her. Ailee contemplated her impending operation and the undeniable risks attached to a major operation. A long anaesthetic, and after, living the rest of her life with only one kidney. Not huge risks statistically but risks nevertheless.

There were physical restrictions for the first few months post-surgery, and changes in body image she would have to come to terms with, like a scar and tenderness. And a slightly greater risk in pregnancy if she was so lucky later in her life.

Her teenage brother's deteriorating health was more important than everything at this time, a decision she'd make every day of her life, to stay on standby until the timing was medically perfect for him to be a recipient of her kidney.

Then Fergus had mentioned how difficult his relationship with his daughter had become – no doubt she was terrified something would happen to her father. Ailee couldn't expose them to the next few months of her life. To the prospect of bringing back all Simone's memories of her mother's death with her own impending operation.

And if she'd told Fergus upfront...

In reality he wouldn't want her to. No matter how much she could dream at this moment, she knew she would have reservations later on, and so would he. Fergus would probably have reservations as soon as he woke up.

Though he had said, *"What if this is our one chance? This could be the start of something special, Ailee. Do you feel that?"* The words he'd spoken had fitted so well with what had gone between them and what she'd most wanted to hear, but in the pale light of the clock illumination, a clock in a stranger's bedroom, she couldn't allow herself to listen to him or acknowledge his power over her.

It would be better to stop now and see what the future held, if anything, when her family commitments had been met.

Ailee looked across at the sleeping man, his face gentle in repose, and her eyes stung with loss from even this brief a connection. She couldn't tell her family about Fergus either.

Her mother and brother would say that they couldn't risk her early relationship with Fergus and call off the whole thing again.

It had taken her so long to get through to her family that she didn't consider donating her kidney a sacrifice. It was a privilege to be able to so vastly improve her brother's quality of life at such little personal cost.

'Fergus, I'm sorry,' she whispered on a soft breath and swallowed the tears in her throat.

Ailee rose, dressed and scribbled briefly on the embossed hotel notepad beside the bed. Shivering, she let herself out.

It felt surreal to come from a stranger's hotel room, dressed in her day clothes, her lips still swollen from his kisses and the scent of him still on her clothes. She should have been wrapped in his arms until their flight early tomorrow morning.

After a scalding shower that didn't warm her, Ailee lay and stared at the ceiling. She half expected him to ring her or knock at her door with a question about dinner. She wasn't hungry, or sleepy, so climbed back out of bed.

She booked her reminder call for the flight and went back to working on her report, ears strained for a knock.

It was six a.m. Eastern Standard Time when Ailee's flight docked at Sydney airport's Terminal One, and their aircraft must have been one of the morning's first arrivals as the big hall wasn't crowded. With no heavy luggage, Ailee passed quickly through immigration and customs and she came out into the arrivals hall to see her mother waiting for her.

Helen Green stood tall like her daughter, her faded red hair a rosy blonde, and her face lit with the loving smile that had healed a hundred skinned knees over the decades. Ailee hugged her mother for comfort. The scent of fresh scones and rosemary soap made her shoulders sag with instant comfort as she was hugged strongly back. It was so good to see her.

Ailee stepped back, still holding her mum's arms. 'Where's William?'

Her mother met her concerned look with one of her own. 'In hospital. I'll tell you in the car.'

Ailee's heart sank. 'Let's get out of here, then.' She didn't want to look around to see if anyone was meeting Fergus. To risk the awkwardness of running into him.

Helen paused and turned to study her daughter searchingly. 'Are you well?'

'Fine. Just tired, that's all.' Ailee fiddled with her tote bag, checking she'd replaced her passport and zipped it closed again. Diverting herself and hopefully her mum. She didn't want to see the concerned look from her mother, or admit that her mother could look deep into her heart and divine there was more bothering her than a red-eye flight. 'William would have enjoyed the bustle of the airport,' she said to divert more attention away from herself.

She remembered the souvenirs, different coloured singing bagpipes that would drive her mother mad and forced a smile.

'Come on, Mum. I need a cup of your tea and I've presents to distribute.'

Chapter 8

Fergus

Fergus heard the click of the hotel room door and his hand slid across and found the warmth of the sheets next to him instead of the warmth of Ailee's body.

He shuddered at the sense of loss that swept over him. 'Ailee?' He looked towards the bathroom but the door was open the large expanse of space echoing with emptiness.

She'd gone. Just like that. After the day they'd shared. After sleeping with her hand in his.

He shook his head, unable to believe she'd slipped away without a word. Fled. Yes, that was the word he sought.

He hadn't picked that in her but he knew he'd pushed fast and inexplicably and he shouldn't have been surprised. He'd been too desperate to cling to the sunshine she projected, the idea they were fated and had found each other.

The unexpected fantasy turned into an illusion.

He knew she'd gone, but he found final confirmation when he sat on the edge of the bed and his glance fell on the note she'd written.

'Dear Fergus, Thank you for the day. Ailee.'

That was it? Nothing else? No personal touch, no reflection of her vibrant personality, no touch of humour.

No phone number. No meet in Sydney. No future plans.

He remembered the way she'd first ignored him in the plane, and he wished bitterly that she hadn't turned to him a few minutes later. That he hadn't asked her to talk.

Obviously their time together had left no impression on her, while he feared she'd pierced the protective shell he'd sworn to keep intact — and he wasn't sure the wound would heal at all well.

How could such a short encounter affect him so deeply?

When he landed at Sydney airport Fergus handed his carry-on over to his driver and scanned the arrivals hall until he caught a disappearing glimpse of Ailee as she left with an older woman. He would recognise her anywhere. Now.

Disappointment made his breath catch. He'd seen nothing of her since she'd left his room in Singapore, neither at their hotel or the airport. He'd intended to arrange an upgrade for her on that final flight, but after her cool exit from his room and that cold little bedside note, he hadn't thought she wanted him near her. He left well-enough alone.

So he'd travelled the last leg in the pointy end of the plane with Ailee back in Economy, and he guessed that was lucky because if he'd had to sit and watch her for eight hours, he would have weakened and reached out with a suggestion they meet at least one more time.

He hated weakness, especially in himself.

Fergus sighed and followed his driver from the terminal to the car park. It was better to suffer a little now because if watching her leave was this bad after one flight and one short day in Singapore, then long-term exposure to the woman could be fatal.

A sudden uneasy thought finally pierced his tired brain and made him wonder why he hadn't thought of it before. What if there was another reason she hadn't stayed? What if Ailee was sick, had been ill, or would be? What if she was awaiting medical results that could prove life-altering?

He shook his head. He'd never seen anyone healthier or more physically fit the woman who had strode around Singapore in the equatorial heat, her smile bright, her energy never flagging? His groin clenched and he gritted his teeth.

It was astonishing but egotistical of him that their time together hadn't been as special for her as it had been for him. Should he have pushed his advantage when he'd had it? No. He'd seen something more precious than a one-night stand in Ailee's company. Clearly, he'd been mistaken or totally missed her reasons for her flight.

He lacked practice in the art of wooing women but he'd have sworn he'd connected with Ailee during their time together. Connected on a level beyond physical desire.

He was a fool and a besotted one at that.

Enough. He had to let her go.

He and Simone made a good team. He might check with his daughter again to find out if the boarding-school thing was working, though. If one good thing came from his brief encounter with Ailee, that could be it.

Chapter 9

Ailee

In her mother's car, Ailee cast one final look at the passengers streaming from the terminal into the car park and then she faced the front. 'So how is William?'

'He's had a bad week. His creatinine level is sky high and his electrolytes are all over the place.'

Her mother's voice was heavy with concern and Ailee could see the strain in the set of her mouth. The small tick above her cheek. Helen went on. 'He's so weak he can only take two hours of dialysis for the next few days. Hopefully he'll be able to build up his tolerance and extend the length to gain strength for the operation.'

Ailee pressed her hand on her mother's leg in comfort.

'He'll pull through, Mum. He's a fighter.'

Helen swallowed. 'It's been terrible, watching him. He's so young for this.' Ailee could hear the tremor in her mother's voice as she listened.

She'd left all this on her mother's shoulders. But she'd had such an opportunity to gain experience they'd all decided she had to have this sabbatical to London for her career. While she could. But this she needed to hear. 'Tell me.'

'The body rash had been the worst, but he's so tired and nauseous. Now the convulsions, and I think they'll decide on your transplant in the next few weeks if he can get well enough to undergo the operation.'

'That's a good thing.' Ailee's voice was firm with conviction. She wanted to do this, see her brother well, and to help her mother's greatest fears be put aside.

'I can't wait for it all to be over. For William to get his life back. To see energy and colour in his face will be worth everything.' Even Fergus. 'He's eighteen, for heaven's sake. He should be out chasing girls.'

A sudden snapshot of Fergus, his eyes black with desire, his hands on her and hers on him, made her squeeze her hands in her lap, and she was glad that her mother was driving and couldn't hear her tiny gasp for what might have been, but the thought was fleeting. Not now. It would never have worked now.

William was the important one. Thank goodness she'd left Fergus when she did.

After a day forcing herself to stay focused on tasks she needed to complete after being away for three months, and finally in her pyjamas ready for bed at a normal hour for Australia, her mother came to Ailee's room. 'I'm still not convinced you should do this, darling.'

Ailee hugged her and sat her down on the bed beside her. 'Look, Mum, the only drawback I can see is no contact sport, and I was never that good at netball anyway.'

She tried to lighten her mother's concerns with that touch of humour and earned a hint of a smile for her effort.

'I will always have to wear a seat belt in the car in case of accidents but I would have anyway.' She ticked this concern off on her fingers. 'Diet and exercise are not something I have a problem with, except for the occasional chocolate biscuit.'

Both women smiled because Ailee's weakness for chocolate-covered biscuits was a joke in the family.

Helen chewed her lip. 'What about childbearing? When you get married?'

'If I get married! I'm nearly thirty and no knight on a charger has chatted me up yet.' She looked away. Now, that was the first lie she'd ever told her mother!

Helen missed her daughter's lack of conviction. 'But he's out there somewhere. With one kidney there is some increase of risk if you became pregnant.'

'Mother.' Ailee grasped Helen gently by the shoulders and looked into her worried eyes. 'We both want William well. Some people are born with one kidney and never have a moment's problem. I could get hit by a bus tomorrow and lose a kidney or worse. Even someone who's had a kidney transplant can have a baby. We've been all through this.' She touched her mother's cheek and lowered her voice. 'I'm sure this is what I want.'

Helen couldn't hide the relief that warred with her worry. 'I'm so proud of you, Ailee.'

'Fiddle.' Ailee thought little of pride when her brother's health was at stake. 'If the roles were reversed, William would do the same for me like a shot. Stop worrying about it and let's concentrate on getting William well enough to undergo the transplant so we can all finally relax.'

A week later, Ailee looked round her temporary coordinator's office at Sydney West, one of the two major transplant hospitals in New South Wales, and then settled into the worn black swivel chair and switched on her computer.

Transplant co-ordinators didn't have much down time and when the transitory vacancy had been difficult to fill, Ailee had offered to fill the gap until the replacement sister arrived in two weeks, as a favour to her boss. Ailee was way over-qualified as a surgeon instead of a nurse, but the experience would stand her in good stead when she gained her own consultancy.

She believed so passionately in the donor programme she could only benefit from access to another facet of the process and anticipated the day when she saw her brother William energetic and happy. Hopefully, that day wasn't far away.

As temporary transplant co-ordinator, Ailee would not only be responsible for the care and preparation of the computer-chosen patients needing organ donation but also for liaison with the families of donors who had been fatally injured and had allowed their organs to be harvested, and, of course, with live donors themselves recovering from the life-saving operations.

She would be the one who interacted with relatives in regard to any organ donation and the arrangement of the organ-donation procedure. Afterwards she would follow up with the families and inform them of the progress of any of the recipients who had benefited from their relative's generous act.

While incumbent, even if briefly when their own operation came forward in time, she hoped to help raise the profile of people signing organ-donation cards. For the moment she needed to grab the patient list and head over to the kidney transplant unit for the morning's ward round. As well as the head of department, Dr Lewis Harry, she knew most of the team of surgeons, physicians, nurses, pharmacists and dieticians who kept the new recipients in optimum health.

As Ailee entered the airy ward, there was a vibrancy about the unit that made her pause so that she had a moment to study the group of professionals up ahead before they saw her. Something was different.

Disbelieving, rocked to her core, almost unable to take it in, she saw the big man at the centre of the group. Heat rushed into her face.

What was *he* doing here?

The last week had felt like a lifetime, but one lingering look at Fergus McVicker brought back Singapore so poignantly her body shuddered as if he'd touched her again. It hadn't been as easy as she'd hoped to go on and not regret Fergus, and he'd shared her dreams every night in her lonely bed as if to drive home the fact.

Now the real man confronted her and this was the last thing she needed on the first day of her temporary post. So much for doing the ward a favour.

Ailee searched the rest of the team, all known to her from her visits here with William, but the delightful Dr Harry was missing. The consultant who had recruited her for the job, and would care for both William and her, had promised to be here for her first morning.

There wasn't time to dwell on this shock because Fergus had looked up and was staring across at her. There was no mercy in his look. He didn't look surprised, so at least one of them had known in advance about this meeting.

Ailee lifted her chin and crossed the room. 'Good morning, everyone. For those who aren't aware, I'm the temporary transplant co-ordinator while Maureen's broken arm is mending and before the replacement sister can start.'

Ailee ignored the icy gaze fixed on her by Fergus as her colleagues murmured their appreciation. Fergus finally looked away and Ailee breathed a tiny sigh of relief. She would have to deal with him later, though she had no idea how, as he'd obviously taken her rapid exit from his room in the worst possible way.

Hopefully she would be more prepared when the time for discussion came.

'Now that Dr Green has arrived, we'll get on with the round, shall we?' There was no hesitation at the end of the sentence and Fergus set off with his entourage in tow.

The tiny note of censure in his comment made Ailee lift her brows in surprise but she shrugged it off. She'd been on time. What was his problem?

Maurice, the new young pharmacist, walked beside Ailee and she quietly asked the question uppermost in her mind. 'Where's Dr Harry?'

'His wife had a stroke last night, and McVicker has been seconded from Sydney East to cover for the next few weeks. We're lucky. He's a leader in the field and just back from Britain, like you.'

'Poor Mrs Harry.' A kinder, more pleasant woman would be difficult to find. That kind of luck they could both do without.

Which left her with Fergus. Inwardly Ailee sighed. She seemed destined to come up against this man in her life at a time that wasn't at all convenient.

'Are you with us, Dr Green?' This time the question was pointed and beside her she could feel the surprise emanating from Maurice. The young pharmacist raised his eyebrows at her in silent query. Ailee's usually placid temper began a slow burn and she lifted her chin. McVicker didn't need to make such an obvious point of his problem with her.

'Of course, Mr McVicker,' she said calmly, at least on the surface. 'Everyone is here because they want to be.'

Fergus blinked and for a moment she thought he'd smile but he didn't.

Ailee knew the patients they would see today because she'd come in yesterday to read all the notes and introduce herself to them. She'd ignore the consultant and concentrate on the important people in the room.

The young woman in the first bed, Jody Withers, was unable to hide her excitement.

Today was Jody's discharge day, and she'd spent the last two weeks smiling since she'd woken up with her new kidney and pancreas. Jody had been on the waiting list for two years and the double-transplant call had come the day before her twenty-first birthday. She represented a bright star in the sometimes-tragic arena of transplant recipients.

Jody could now forgo the thrice-weekly dialysis for her renal failure, which she'd fitted in after work, and her newly donated pancreas meant she was no longer an insulin-dependent diabetic. The four insulin needles a day she'd lived with since she'd been ten were now a thing of the past.

'So how do you feel, Jody?' It seemed Fergus had also done his homework because Jody was quite at ease with the great man.

'Still blown away that somebody somewhere changed my life by doing this, Mr McVicker.' She closed her eyes briefly and shrugged, her young face suddenly troubled. 'I can't stop thinking about my donor's family giving permission while they dealt with losing someone they loved.'

Ailee empathised with the young woman. This was part of her job. 'We do understand, Jody. It's the thought uppermost in all recipients' minds. Some recipients have said a letter to the donor family feels like it helps. You could write down your feelings and when you're happy with how it sounds we can forward your letter to your donor's family. I really believe it helps them as well to hear how much of a miracle their loved one has made possible.'

Jody's smile looked slightly less strained. 'That would be wonderful, Ailee. I'll bring a letter back when I come in for my check-up next week.'

Ailee sensed Fergus's attention on her again. Not sure where she'd picked up this new freakin' Fergus antenna and cursing it, she forced herself to ignore the sensations that fluttered over her skin. Yup, it was going to be incredibly difficult to work with this man. But if she'd slept with him, it would have been even more so. She smiled sourly at that. She'd just have to keep her distance and ignore the way his presence affected her.

Fergus seemed to be managing more easily than she was, but he'd had prior warning. She would have liked some of that.

She'd probably been a pleasant interlude for him. One who hadn't come through and not what he wanted to find at work. Her stomach sank but she risked a glance under her brows at him, but he was focused on Jody.

His thoughts were where hers should be — on the patient. 'All your pathology results look perfect today, Jody,' Fergus said. 'Are you happy with your medications?'

Jody nodded. 'I have a system for taking them. Maurice has helped me work out a schedule so I feel less sick, and won't forget any of the doses. I just don't want to put on too much weight or get a moon face.'

Fergus smiled at the girl. 'Some side-effects we can help a little with and Louise, the dietician, is here for you any time you need her.'

The smiled dropped but there was kindness in the timbre of his voice. Enough to make Ailee's heart ache just a little.

'You must contact us if you become unwell or you notice change or a decrease in your urine output. Try the ward phone number and if what they suggest doesn't work, this is my card. While Dr Harry is away, you can ring me on my mobile any time if you're worried.'

He passed over a small white card and Ailee was glad to see the relief on Jody's face. It was generous of Fergus to make the gesture. Dr Harry was who they relied on.

The round went on.

In the next room, a young couple were scheduled for surgery the next day. Peter was donating one of his kidneys to Emma, his wife.

Emma, blonde-haired and blue-eyed, had become extremely ill with pregnancy-induced hypertension during the birth of their twin daughters. Emma's blood pressure had been so high and uncontrollable that she had irretrievably damaged both her kidneys.

Three months later she had reached end-stage kidney failure and the thrice-weekly dialysis had been a constant juggling act for their small family. If all went well, tomorrow's operation would return their shattered lives to some degree of normality and Emma and Peter were looking forward to more quality time with their daughters.

'A final day of work-up and then the big day.' Fergus looked across at Emma who smiled back weakly. His voice lowered. 'How are you, Emma?'

'Worried if anything happens to Peter.' Emma's eyes sparkled with unshed tears and she put her hand to her mouth so it was difficult to hear what she said.

Fergus bent towards her and tipped her chin up so she could see his smile. 'We'll be taking special care of him. Your Peter has three women who need him and I know he can't wait to see some colour in the cheeks of the woman he loves.'

Emma nodded and Fergus went on. 'Now, save some sympathy for yourself. You'll be under the anaesthetic longer than Peter and I want you to rest as much as you can today.'

Peter spoke from the next bed, where he was sitting fully dressed. He pointed to a picture of two chubby babies in matching pink outfits who grinned toothlessly out of the photo frame. 'My mum brought the girls in last night, so they aren't coming in today.'

Fergus shook hands with him. 'How are you feeling, Peter? Nervous?'

Peter was dark-haired and serious. 'Perhaps a little, but I'm excited, too. Emma and I are a team, and half the team is out on her feet. Normally I can't keep up with her. I want Emma well.'

Ailee lowered her voice. 'Is your mum going to stay for a while to help with the children? You need to rest afterwards and you'll be pretty sore.'

'Yes.' Peter also spoke quietly. 'And my dad's taken over running the store. I worry about his heart condition but we just can't afford to close until I get well enough to go back.'

Fergus nodded and Ailee could see the frustration in his body language. 'That's where everything needs to change. Live donors save lives and save the government hundreds of thousands of dollars in dialysis every year. Donors need their out-of-pocket expenses reimbursed for loss of wages. We're not talking about making a profit but to take away the hardship such a selfless act incurs.'

Peter sighed. 'Wouldn't that make it easier? But if it costs us our home, it's still worth it. We have to have Emma well again.'

'At least with the laparoscopic surgery that I use, your recovery time will be reduced by a few weeks. There will still be four small wounds, one for the laparoscopic camera on its cable to allow me vision for what I'm doing and two for the other instruments that will divide and separate your kidney from its bed. A fourth excision below the umbilicus will be made through which to remove the kidney.'

'It sounds so easy.' Peter rolled his eyes. 'Not!'

'There are still risks but we'll look after you and your wife.' Fergus rested his hand on Peter's shoulder. 'I'll come back tonight and answer any final questions about tomorrow and look at the last lot of results.'

'Maurice—' Fergus patted the pharmacist on the back '—is going to run through Emma's immunosuppressant regime again with you both so we're sure you understand how to help prevent her body rejecting your kidney and the side-effects she can expect. If there's anything else you don't understand, ask Ailee or any of the team, and we'll take some extra time to explain.'

The group moved on and she noticed that Fergus seemed to have a rapport with every patient. She had no idea how he'd had the time if Dr Harry only left last night. This version of Fergus – warm and open and charismatic – reminded her of the man she'd spent time with in Singapore. A world apart from the version who'd greeted her earlier with snark.

When the round was over, the team met in the foyer to discuss any further changes or additions that were needed, and then the group broke up.

'Dr Green?' Fergus spoke quietly but his voice carried effortlessly to her. 'I'd like to speak to you in the office, please.'

She looked up at Fergus's request and met his eyes. His were cool. Ailee's heart gave a thump which she ignored and unobtrusively drew in a deep breath. They were both professionals. Without saying a word she preceded him into the office and he closed the door behind them.

He gestured for her to sit but Ailee shook her head. A discussion that needed a seat, she was not ready for. 'I don't have the time to sit down. What can I do for you, Mr McVicker?'

He stared at a point beyond her left shoulder. 'I apologise for being abrupt and only wish to make it clear you'll have no unwanted attention from me.'

Ailee glanced at the door, eager to get out of there and away from his presence. 'Thank you. Is that all? I gather you were expecting me?'

'Oh, I knew you were here. I won't single you out again —unless you're late. That will be all, thank you, Doctor.'

'As I am never late, that will not be a problem.'

Ailee cast a cool look at him and left the room.

Chapter 10

Fergus

Fergus watched her go, not sure he'd handled that well.

When she'd walked into the ward that morning, her presence had punched him in the gut as it had the first time he'd seen her, but he'd just have to get over that.

Listening to her talk to Jody and Peter reminded him of her warm support on the plane as he'd been dealing with his stupid phobia. Interestingly he'd not even noticed taking off in Singapore. His mind had been so thoroughly entrenched in other "things".

When Lionel Harry had asked him to cover him here, he'd been trapped and unable to refuse. He wasn't scheduled back at his own hospital for a month and was the most likely replacement in an emergency. Those on waiting lists often didn't have a month to wait around.

If he'd known Ailee worked here, he would have flown a replacement in from overseas rather than come himself. Unfortunately, by the time he'd found out he'd already agreed to come.

To top that off, Simone hadn't been impressed that he'd cancelled their holiday, even though she hadn't been eager to spend the time with him either. But he'd make it up to her. At least that decision, to take her out of boarding school, had gone well. Thanks to Ailee's advice. She seemed pleased to be back home as a day student again.

Of course, right on cue, his mind arrowed back to Ailee, as it had several times a day and most of the nights over the last week. He was surprised their paths hadn't crossed before, considering they both worked in the same field. In the same city but different hospitals.

Apparently, she was a gifted surgeon.

He would not have forgotten a previous meeting.

He'd since discovered she was well liked and respected for her dedication to the renal transplant unit. He had yet to discover why she was temping in a transplant co-ordinator's job instead of getting on with resuming her position, but he would find out.

Not that he'd be a fool again with this woman. He just wanted to know why she'd made such a puzzling career move.

When the rounds were due to start again, he found himself watching for her, senses alert, despite carrying on conversations with the other professionals around him.

He glanced at his watch. Three minutes until they were due to start. The transplant assessment clinic was where the renal team reviewed the suitability of end-stage renal patients for transplantation.

Seems he'd suddenly developed a fetish for punctuality.

Again, when Ailee arrived at the ward, two minutes early, everyone else was already assembled. She saw him glance at the clock and she lifted her chin to meet his gaze. Raised her brows at him. She wasn't late.

William Green was the first patient and when Fergus picked up the chart his brow furrowed as he read the name. Green. Not really ironic. Green was a common name. But reminders of Ailee Green seemed to be everywhere.

He shut the thoughts off. 'Hello, William. I see you've just been through a tough patch but are improving steadily now. How are you feeling today?'

'I'm getting there.' He was a tall boy and there was something familiar about him that Fergus couldn't quite pin down. He'd probably seen him at another renal unit but it wasn't like him to forget a face.

'So you have this week and next week in the assessment clinic to finalise dates for your transplant.' He spotted a red flag in the chart. 'I see you've come in consistently over your fluid limit.'

He looked up and the boy's gaze slid away. Trouble?

'Let's get you examined,' he continued, 'and we'll answer any questions you have because I expect your operation could be as early as Monday week if you continue to improve.'

Rita pulled the curtains and the rest of the team stepped back.

Chapter 11

Ailee

So, Fergus hadn't connected William with her.

Ailee felt a twinge of guilt that she hadn't told him, though when could she have done so? Considering how unfriendly he'd been to her, he probably wouldn't care. No, that was unfair. When she wasn't being cross with him for his harshness to her, she knew he would care. About anyone. She could see his attention and concern for every single patient and her instincts said this man would care for her health as well.

Maybe if she'd told him why she left his room in Singapore, he wouldn't be treating her like this. But that was all water under an Oriental bridge.

Today had been huge, considering all that was happening.

Her new job, running into Fergus, William coming in for assessment to set the date for their operations — it was no wonder her head was spinning.

'Are you okay?' Maurice was beside her and his face showed concern.

'I'm fine. Sorry. I suppose I just realised how dangerous the op is for William.'

'William isn't the only person who's having an operation.'

Ailee shook her head. 'Mine's nothing. A bit of discomfort, a scar, and I'll be just as healthy at the end. William has the drugs to live with for the rest of his life.'

'And a much better life he'll have, thanks to you.'

Ailee frowned at Maurice, hoping the pharmacist's quiet voice didn't carry to inside the curtains. And something else she noticed, there was no doubt his look held particular warmth.

She bit back a sigh and a stab of irritation. More complications. She felt a hundred years older than Maurice but he was probably only a year or two younger. Although he was a nice lad, he seemed so young and immature... especially after Singapore.

That did not mean Fergus had already spoiled other men for her. It didn't.

The curtains pulled back and her gaze was drawn to the man in her thoughts who stared straight into her face. His expression was unreadable, tight with some emotion she could feel even if she couldn't understand it. There was a moment's silence and, for a second, she thought he'd discovered William was her brother and he was going to take her arm and steer her into the office.

Her heart pounded in her chest. Two trips to the office would start a gossip storm.

But he didn't.

He just moved on.

And she let out a huff of released breath.

Ailee's day got steadily busier. She had a lecture on donor liaison with medical students at one and it was five to the hour now. All medical professionals needed to be skilled and empathetic when approaching bereaved families, and needed to learn how to discuss organ and tissue donation. To deliver this important lesson her brain couldn't be distracted by thoughts of Fergus McVicker.

The lecture went well and her plug for all who attended to sign donor cards was well received, as was her point that anyone considering such a pledge should also make their family aware of it.

Ailee knew this was one of the most common stumbling blocks between the original intent of the donor and the recipient's life being saved.

Afternoon tea was a snatched sandwich in place of lunch and just enough time to ask Rita, the charge nurse of the renal transplant unit, the burning question, 'How long is Fergus McVicker staying?'

'What's the story with you two?' Rita's bright blue eyes stared straight at Ailee while she avoided the question.

Ailee raised her brows and stared right back, a trick she'd learned from her brother when he was cornered. 'There's no story. He must have taken an instant dislike to me.'

Rita laughed, the sound rich and delighted, and it spilled down the corridor at the idiocy of that comment. 'Nobody takes an instant dislike to you. Look at you! Care and empathy shine out of every gorgeous pore.'

'Please, Rita. Give me the good news.'

Rita shrugged and gave. 'He's here for two weeks minimum, four weeks max. It all depends on Mrs Harry. She's improving well and she may visit their daughter for her convalescence, in which case Dr Harry will be back sooner.'

'So how could our Mr McVicker drop everything at Sydney East?'

'Holidays. Apparently, he's got a daughter who isn't happy Daddy's taken on the job, though. He's a widower and unattached. He could be just your type, Ailee, when all this is over.' Ailee looked at Rita and rolled her eyes. But she could feel herself blushing.

Rita narrowed her eyes knowingly. Smiled. 'Oh, my. Things are going to be interesting around here this next few weeks.'

By Wednesday Ailee had found her feet in her new job and the minutae of end tying she hadn't known as a surgeon that went on behind the scenes filled her with admiration for the previous coordinator. Each new challenge served to increase her respect for the whole renal team.

At the top of her admiration list, surprisingly, was Fergus McVicker, tireless in his pursuit of optimum health for his patients and demanding high standards from all on the team. The fact that he received unqualified support from everyone he came into contact with was largely due to his own dedication.

The patients adored him and Ailee found it hard to comprehend that she had shared such intimacy with this driven man who barely had time to eat and obviously didn't sleep.

Superficially she appeared the most immune out of the staff to seeing Fergus almost every day.

Unfortunately, she couldn't help the jump in her heart rate or ache in her chest when she was near him, and she sometimes wondered if she would go quietly insane for wanting some of their closeness to return.

If only William's operation could be scheduled sooner and she could try to salvage some rapport from their past association afterwards. Before it was too late for them.

But life was sometimes like that. Oblivious to mortals. Contrary.

An hour after the assessment clinic, Ailee's pager went off. The call originated from Intensive Care to call her for donor liaison. ICU had a family who hadn't known their mortally injured daughter had signed a donor card. The girl's parents were naturally having trouble coming to terms with her wish to donate her organs.

Ailee's stomach fluttered at the thought of the hours ahead. Her input could make such a difference to their decision, many people's lives, and especially the donor family's grieving process, and she was anxious to do her best.

When Ailee arrived at the intensive care unit, Andrew, an anaesthetist she'd worked with the previous year, handed her the second set of tragic brain-stem tests from the unfortunate young woman.

'Hey, Ailee. Good to see you back, but not in these circumstances. I have heartbreak here for you. Twenty-five-year old Eva Ellis was involved in a car accident and never regained consciousness.' They both looked towards the separate room adjacent to the desk.

Andrew went on quietly. 'Her parents are with her. In shock, of course.' His pager went off and he glanced down at the screen. 'Sorry. I have to go.' He patted Ailee on the back. 'Good luck.'

Eva's parents were sitting beside the bed, holding their daughter's hand in a three-person grip – though one of the participants had no lifeforce in her clasp. Ailee's throat tightened as she crossed to the nurse who was specialling Eva on the ventilator.

The machine breathed and hissed mechanically to provide inflation and oxygen to a person who would never recover, who would never breathe or think for herself again.

The tragedy felt heartrending and her voice was quiet as she addressed the nurse. 'I'm Ailee Green, the transplant co-ordinator.'

The nurse was very young but remarkably composed. 'It's Dr Green, isn't it? I'm Sam. The family are waiting to speak to you. I told them you'd be here soon. I'll introduce you.'

Sam took Ailee across to the grieving parents. 'Excuse me, Mr and Mrs Ellis. This is Dr Green. She's the transplant co-ordinator we spoke about who can answer your questions.'

A grief-ravaged woman in her early fifties held out her hand and her fingers trembled in Ailee's grip with the force of her will not to cry. 'I'm Marion. This is my husband, John.'

Ailee squeezed the woman's hand. 'I'm Ailee. I'm so sorry to meet you in these circumstances and to intrude on your grief at this time. The fact that your daughter has signed and carried a donor card tells us a little about how special a person she was.'

She let that hang in the air.

The words were important. Respectful. Admiring. 'I know this is very hard to discuss but I will try to keep it as simple as possible.'

Marion blinked tears away and Ailee went on. 'I understand you and your husband didn't know that Eva had signed a donor card?'

Both parents shook their head.

'So you were shocked?'

Marion nodded. 'It wasn't something we'd ever talked about. Now, seeing Eva like this...' Her voice broke before she composed herself with a deep shuddering breath. 'It   would be like killing our own daughter to give away her organs. We don't know what to do.'

'It's understandable for you think that way.' Ailee's voice was very soft, very gentle. She reached out and took Marion's hand. 'You both know that the person you knew as Eva, your daughter, has gone. She can't ever come back except in your memories. Her brain has suffered such a loss of oxygen that it cannot even tell her body to breathe for her.'

Ailee looked at the machine, and Eva's parents followed her gaze. 'If the machine wasn't inflating her lungs, she would have died hours ago.'

Ailee stopped to let her words sink in. She couldn't imagine the pain these parents must be going through at this moment, and for a second she doubted she could control her own emotions.

Then she thought of Jody — a young woman with her whole life ahead of her, except she'd needed a new kidney and pancreas — and how the incredible gift bestowed by her donor and their family had changed her life.

Ailee lifted her chin. Blinked away the stinging in her eyes and drew a breath. Surely it was unnecessary to waste Eva's perfectly functioning organs when Eva herself had seen the value in the concept.

'If I could share something with you. To give you a different perspective?'

Eva's parents both inclined their heads.

'We had a young woman on our transplant ward who went home this week. She is a wonderfully genuine and intelligent young woman, much like I imagine your daughter was, and has a lovely sense of humour. Only a month ago she was dying—' Ailee slowed for them to take this in '—because her kidneys had both stopped working and dialysis was making her sicker. She's had severe diabetes since she was ten.'

Marion said, 'Eva had a school friend with diabetes. With the needles.'

'Then you know what this means.'

Eva's mother waved for her to go on.

'On Monday this young woman went home with not only a new kidney but a new pancreas as well. Amazingly, she isn't even a diabetic now. This young woman's life is possible because of wonderful people like you and your daughter who have made the decision to donate their organs after they have died.'

'Does the donor—' Marion stumbled over the word '—does her family get to meet the person who has their relative's organs?'

Ailee shook her head. 'Not usually. But this woman I mentioned is writing a letter that I will pass on to the family. Of all the people who know what a huge thing this is for the donor family to agree to, the recipients are the most aware. They actually find it very hard to get over how fortunate they are.'

'We've been trying to reconcile this and that helps. Thank you.' Marion turned to her husband who nodded back. 'Eva was a very caring person. She would hate to think we wasted her organs when she didn't need them any more.'

John spoke for the first time. 'We can't let our little girl down on this, Marion.' The balding man's eyes were brimming with tears. 'It's what she wanted and it's the last thing we can do for our baby.'

Ailee's eyes stung again. For these amazing people. 'If you both agree, Eva's donation will help a lot of people — not just one or two. In a week or so I will let you know just how much your daughter's donation is going to change the lives of so many people.'

Marion blew her nose and sniffed. 'How does it happen?' And then, 'Will you be there?'

'I won't be in the actual operating room, but I will be co-ordinating from the outside. I can arrange for you to speak to someone who will be at the operation, though.'

Marion looked at her husband and their eyes met and held. 'Yes. Please. I think we need that.'

'I'll arrange that. We also need to know if there are any organs or tissue restrictions you would like me to pass on to the transplant team. Some people do have restrictions and we respect that.'

Marion looked across at John and he shook his head slowly. 'They can take whatever will help someone else. The real essence of our daughter is free. She doesn't need her body now.'

'I'll come back this evening after I've organised the teams and set up the paperwork. We need to have blood taken for tissue-typing and other checks.' Eva's parents dipped their heads. 'And we need you to fill out a questionnaire to ask about her general health. Nurse will help you with that.'

Ailee contacted the transplant data office and the patient's details were entered. The computer assimilated the information and allocated the organs to those most in need and who were compatible.

There was one phone call she was dreading. She'd run through who on the transplant or harvest team she would contact to meet Eva's parents, and the most obvious choice was the man in charge. Ailee had no doubt that despite Fergus's behaviour towards her at the moment, he would be a very caring advocate to introduce to the grieving parents.

'Mr McVicker? It's Ailee Green. I'm sorry to bother you at your surgery but I have a favour to ask.'

'Yes, Ailee?' There was an expectant note in his voice but she was too anxious to try and figure it out.

'The family of the young woman donor who was admitted today would like to speak to someone who will be present during the operation. Would you speak to them for me, please, before you scrub?'

'Of course. I'll meet them in ICU at seven. Is that all?'

Ailee sighed with relief. 'Yes, thanks,' she said, and as she tried to put the phone down she realised she'd have to consciously release her fingers because she'd been gripping the receiver far too fiercely.

Seven. She'd be home late tonight then.

The afternoon passed swiftly and it had been dark for an hour when Ailee returned with Fergus to meet the parents.

'This is Mr McVicker. He's the renal surgeon and in charge of the transplants in this hospital.'

Fergus shook hands with Marion and John. 'Please, accept my sincere commiseration for the tragic loss of your daughter and the difficult and awful situation you are both in.'

Marion swallowed visibly and Fergus went on, 'I want you to know that the operation is performed with every respect and dignity by each of the very experienced transplant teams who will come to our hospital.'

Eva's parents nodded.

'The operations are carried out as sterile operations, of course. Afterwards we do repair any incisions we make as neatly as in all operations.'

Fergus answered a few more questions and then it was time for him to go to theatre.

Marion and John went once more into Intensive Care, heads bowed, weighed down by the magnitude of saying their final goodbye to Eva. 'Will we be able to see Eva's body after the operation?'

Ailee nodded. 'Tomorrow morning I'll come and take you to our chapel in the mortuary, where you can spend as much time as you wish.'

'Thank you, Ailee.'

Ailee swallowed the lump in her throat, her face schooled to show nothing but compassion and control. 'Thank you. You have made the right decision. We all appreciate your kindness during your immense grief. Your daughter's legacy will live on through those she helps.'

'We know. It's just hard to think of it at the moment.' Marion squeezed her husband's hand and Ailee bit her lip.

'Of course. This isn't the time to worry about that. Please, try and get some rest. I'll see you in the morning. Just remember that this is what Eva wanted, but it takes courage from everyone to make this decision.'

Marion looked sadly at Ailee. 'We don't feel brave, just heartbroken.'

Ailee watched them walk away arm in arm, leaning on each other, and she allowed the tears to well in her eyes. Just for a second before she brushed her hand across her face to stem the flow, at least until she reached the safety of her office. But as she pushed open the door the heartbreak overwhelmed her and she sobbed against the closed door.

'I knew you'd be upset,' Fergus said softly from within.

Fergus leant against the wall and had pushed himself off when she entered. He held open his arms and her brain said no as her heart steered her into the comfort of his embrace. His scent, spicy and masculine and familiar, surrounded her with comfort. Just comfort.

She sobbed quietly for a minute to ease the strain of staying strong for the last few hours, and he just held her gently until the storm passed. She had no idea Marion and John's grief had affected her so much. Perhaps there'd been more emotional impact because she was now so personally invested, with William's and her upcoming ops. And her mother's difficult last few months.

'I'm sorry if you think I'm unprofessional. This isn't the first time I've dealt with loved ones, though not as the coordinator of consents and consistent close family contact. Something about Eva's mother affected me.'

'Shhh,' Fergus said quietly. 'Being upset is human and you were totally professional until you closed your door. There is no shame in that.'

Despite her tears, and the embarrassment of letting go, she did feel better and Ailee lifted her ravaged face to thank him, but that thought caught and died as they stared at each other. There was nothing either of them could do as a force greater than their wills drew them together for a single, healing kiss.

His mouth felt undemanding, gentle and healing, but still hot and heavenly, and her body softened into him for a few wonderful moments before reality forced her back.

She could not do this here, now, with him. It was so inappropriate, so unprofessional.

'No.' Ailee stepped back out of his arms and her hand came up to cover her mouth. 'You said this wouldn't happen.'

'I did, didn't I?' Fergus looked at her and again she couldn't read the expression on his face. 'I'm sorry,' he said, and walked out of the office.

She felt like crying again, for a different reason.

The next morning, Thursday, when Ailee went to meet Marion and John to take them to the mortuary, Fergus was with them. He had his arm around Marion, whose face looked ravaged by tears.

Fergus looked so put-together, instead of having operated all night, and only the lines around his eyes betrayed his tiredness.

As Ailee drew closer she could hear no weariness in his voice.

'You can ring my surgery if you have any other questions and I'll phone you back as soon as I can.'

He looked up. His eyes darkened with concern when he saw Ailee, as if he knew how hard this was for her, and she was transported back to their kiss yesterday and how he'd caught her at her most vulnerable.

Then he looked away and she felt cold.

How did he do that?

Fergus spoke to the bereaved parents. 'Here's Dr Green. I have to go but I will leave you in her capable hands.' He shook hands with John and to Ailee's surprise hugged Marion. 'It's been a privilege meeting you both.'

They all watched Fergus move away and John reached over and took his wife's hand. He looked at Ailee and then the sign that pointed the way to the chapel. 'Let's say goodbye to our daughter, love.'

By the time Ailee made it back to the ward she felt emotionally shattered by sharing Marion and John's grief again.

After the last twenty-four hours she admired the injured Maureen, the woman she was replacing at the moment, more than ever. Dealing constantly with such emotive issues, day in and day out, as a transplant co-ordinator was proving more difficult than she could have imagined. So much easier to be the surgeon.

As soon as she walked into the ward her pager went off, just as Rita appeared breathlessly beside her.

'Ailee.' Rita gulped air. 'Mr McVicker is looking for you. The page is from the operating theatres. Emma is bleeding and they need more help. The extra team had to leave and are tied up in a critical trauma case down in Emergency. Fergus wants to know if you can assist in Theatre Six.'

Ailee felt her stomach drop at the thought of Emma, mother of the baby twins, with a major haemorrhage. 'Answer the page. I'm on my way.'

Ailee turned and ran out the door. She didn't bother waiting for the lifts. It was only two flights and the stairwell came out beside the operating suite. She'd surgically assisted Dr Harry there for twelve months before going off to Scotland and she knew the way.

Ailee pushed through the plastic doors. Ominously, there was no one in the reception area. It seemed everyone was caught up with the emergency.

She slipped into the change room and swapped into her theatre scrubs faster than she'd ever done in her life.

When she entered the scrub room to wash up, a spare gown and two pairs of gloves were waiting for her, and before she'd finished drying her hands the scout nurse came in to tie her gown.

'What's happening?' Ailee struggled with her gloves while the nurse finished tying her gown.

'Don't know. The transplanted kidney was seated and blood supply established and everything was routine. The other surgeon left for the emergency downstairs, but then Mr McVicker suspected a hidden bleeder and the new registrar hasn't enough experience to be the help he needs.

'Mr McVicker asked for help and the anaesthetist — you know how Andrew likes to bend the rules — said there was no one else except you. The kidney is at risk, let alone the patient.'

'Nice to be the last hope.' Ailee was finished and spun around to enter the theatre.

'You had our vote.' The nurse glanced through the window into the theatre to make sure the way was clear for the sterile-gowned Ailee to enter.

'You're finally here.' Fergus looked up and his expression appeared grim.

'What can I do?' Ailee answered calmly as she stood beside the shaking registrar and peered into the wound that was awash with bright blood.

'I need some vision through this blood and with only two of us we don't have enough hands.'

'I'll take the sucker.' Ailee spoke to the registrar who thankfully handed over the plastic nozzle. 'You take the retractor and pull from that angle with two hands. It will be easier now.' The young man straightened his shoulders and nodded.

'More swabs.' Fergus stared with narrowed eyes into the wound and Ailee took swabs from the scrub sister, who looked pale under her eye shield as she hurried to do what she was told.

'And can I have a swab on a stick as well, please, when you're ready?' Ailee's gentle voice seemed to dissipate the tension in the room as the scrub sister looked at her with relief.

Ailee swabbed the area she'd just suctioned and for a brief instant a welling of blood could be isolated from the rest before it disappeared under a tide of red that filled the cavity again. 'There.'

'Good work, Ailee.' Fergus had seen it, too, and now that he knew where the problem lay, he set to isolating the vessel as fast as he could.

'Blood pressure's going through the floor.' Andrew's voice drifted laconically to the surgeons as he set about increasing the amount of fluid he was infusing. 'I'm on the last packed cells now.'

'I can see the bleeder.' Fergus acknowledged he'd heard the warning. 'I won't be long and we'll stop wasting the stuff.'

The alarms sounded from the anaesthetic equipment and Ailee spared a brief thought for Peter and Emma's baby girls if Emma's lack of blood caused her to go into cardiac arrest on the table. It was a horrific scenario to contemplate.

She forced away the thought. The situation was grim but she didn't doubt that Fergus would gain control. He had almost finished repairing the vessel, and Ailee had never seen one ligated so well under such circumstances. 'That was quick, but there's still too much blood.'

'Then find where it's coming from, fast.' Fergus finished his knot and held his hand out for another suture.

Ailee spoke to the registrar. 'Can you pull from a more lateral angle? I want to see under the bladder.' For the briefest moment, after suctioning and a quick swipe with the swab at the end of the long forceps, Ailee spotted another mini-fountain of blood. 'There.'

That explained it and she knew they'd win the battle now.

'Saw it. Got it.' Fergus pressed his finger on the spot and collected another swab from the scrub sister. 'You little bastard,' he said softly.

Ailee raised her eyebrows. 'Language.'

The registrar looked doubtfully at Ailee taking on the boss, especially after the morning he'd had. Fergus glanced up in time to see her censure and his eyes crinkled as he relaxed. 'Smack me later.'

Andrew looked up and then adjusted another gauge on his machine as he coughed to hide his amusement. 'So are you people going to be long?'

Fergus had tied off the last of the rogue vessels. 'Closing now.'

Over the next ten minutes Emma's blood pressure crept up and the abdominal layers were closed without further setbacks. Ailee stepped back as the final closure began and stripped off her gloves.

'Thank you, Dr Green.' Fergus didn't take his eyes off the patient but his voice raised the awareness between them.

'My pleasure, Mr McVicker.'

She smiled at the registrar. 'Well done, Tom. It's all good experience afterwards, isn't it?' The registrar looked like he was going to faint. 'Go get a drink of water.'

Ailee stripped off her outer gown to leave the bloodstained clothing in the theatre. She waved at Andrew and smiled at each person in the room except Fergus before she pushed open the door. 'Bye, everybody.'

Ailee didn't go back to the ward. She sat in her office and pretended to do paperwork as her mind kept going over the crisis in theatre.

To lose Emma would have been a horrible, disastrous tragedy, and it had been close. Fergus had been exceptional, very talented. The bleeder had been no one's fault and the spotting of it before closure would have made the difference to trying to retrieve an irretrievable situation if they'd missed it.

When William's transplant was over she would be able to go back to what she loved doing. Be a part of the magic of restoring function to the human body, something she was skilled at and felt passionate about, and there would always be hospitals to take her. Dr Harry had already offered her tenure, working with an eye to a consultancy in the not-too-distant future.

The problem was now that she'd worked with Fergus, it would seem flat. From only that brief window she'd seen skills that she hoped to emulate one day. And that was a whole new kettle of Asian jumping worms.

She picked up the phone. There was work to do before the rounds started.

Chapter 12

Fergus

Fergus knew the moment Ailee arrived on the ward. He tried not to glance her way but it was hard, especially after yesterday.

He'd heard about her skill as a surgeon, he had asked, and that had been backed up by her quiet confidence and skill in the OT. He attributed a portion of the retrieval of Emma's haemorrhage to Ailee's help. It seemed his Ailee was a good woman to have by his side in a crisis. Except she wasn't his Ailee.

Before coming to theatre she'd already had a tough morning, being there to support Eva's grieving parents again and he had no doubt she'd give everything in her work.

Which reminded him, considering her undoubted skill in surgery, it was even more ludicrous she was temping as a co-ordinator.

He had to ask Rita, the unit manager, when he had a chance. But for now there was work. There was always work.

Peter was back from his operation, still groggy from the anaesthetic and pain relief. He opened his eyes and squinted up at Fergus. 'How's Emma, Doc?'

'Emma's doing well. She lost more blood than we anticipated but she's fine now. She'll stay in Intensive Care tonight and High Dependency tomorrow, but it all looks good so far. How are you feeling?'

Peter almost smiled. 'Sore. Glad it's over.' His eyelids drooped and his voice faded. Then he forced his eyes open again. 'You're sure Emma's okay?'

'She's fine. The best thing you can do for your partner is to rest and recover. She'll be just as anxious about you when she comes back to the ward.' He watched Peter's eyes close and the young man's concerned face soften. Thank goodness.

Fergus rubbed his eyes. They felt scratchy with lack of sleep after twelve hours of concentrated surgery. He'd head home for the rest of the morning and catch a couple of hours' shut-eye before the afternoon surgery.

When Fergus opened his eyes, Ailee had come up to the group and her concerned look tore at the fabric of his control. He'd love to rest his head on her. But he couldn't.

'Yes, Ailee?' His voice came out much sharper than he'd intended in a knee-jerk reaction to his own weakness.

He saw her recoil from the harshness in his tone and he winced. Held his hand up. 'Sorry.' Now he just sounded gruff. 'Tired.' Lord, what this woman was doing to his emotions. 'Did you want something?'

'There's a call for you. Rita asked me to pass the message on.'

An excuse to leave! Fergus grabbed at the chance. 'I'll come now. After the round, if you have to contact me, I'll be at home. Ring me there.'

Ailee nodded and turned away to answer a question from Maurice about a new patient who'd just arrived.

Fergus was losing his battle to remain aloof with Ailee. Since the time in theatre she'd never been far from his thoughts.

He woke in the morning dreaming of her back in his arms and at work he felt every smile she gave so freely to all except him. This was crazy. He'd have to do something soon or he'd crack.

'Dr Green? Ailee?' Fergus caught up just as Ailee came to the entrance of the renal ward. She jumped and put her hand to her chest as if he'd leapt out in front of her.

Fergus frowned. 'Sorry. Didn't mean to startle you.'

He watched her take a deep, calming breath and unconsciously his hand lifted to lie on her arm in reassurance.

When she looked down at his fingers on her skin, he felt his own gaze drawn as well. It was as if they were both back in Singapore and finally, lightbulb-moment wise, he had an inkling she was just as affected by his proximity as he was by hers. How had he missed that?

'We need to talk.' His words came out with more overtones than he'd intended, but it was a measure of his relief that he had no control over his voice.

Why hadn't he noticed this before? He wanted to back her into a corner of the ward, put his arms on either side of her head — trap her so she couldn't escape — and find out then and there why she had really run away that morning.

Slowly her head came up and she met his look with a fierce one of her own. 'Is it about a patient?'

No use lying. 'No!'

'Then I'm busy.' She glared at him but he didn't believe her this time.

Under her bravado Fergus could feel Ailee's indecision and he stepped closer. 'Give me a time and we'll talk then.'

Fergus suspected if he didn't pin her down now he would have trouble cornering her again. She hesitated and he pounced. 'No is not an option,' he said quietly.

'How unenlightened. I believe no is always an answer for a woman. Or a man for that matter.'

Fergus winced and understood what he'd said was completely inappropriate. Time for appeal. 'You are entirely correct. Let me try again... Ailee, we need to talk. Would this afternoon, when you finish, suit? Please.'

Ailee shook her head. 'I have a family dinner at seven.'

'Could still work. I can pick you up at five from here and we'll find somewhere private, then I'll drop you back.'

Her eyes narrowed. 'Not too private.' Though her voice remained calm and she looked composed, he had the feeling she wasn't as cool as she seemed.

'As you wish,' he said, and watched her nod and turn to walk away from him.

He just hoped he hadn't been mistaken about his instinct or he was going to look even more of a fool.

Chapter 13

Ailee

Ailee sensed Fergus behind her shoulder, not as staggered an arrival as she would have liked, and even though he wasn't touching her, they entered the ward together.

Rita raised her eyebrows and Ailee assumed that everyone else could see the tension between them, too. Thankfully the unit manager didn't make one of her usual teasing comments.

The ward had a new patient today and soon all attention centred on Lawrence Roper.

Lawrence had needed a kidney transplant after going into renal failure a year ago and, because he was an orphan and a single man, and the average waiting time in Australia for a donated kidney was four years, sometimes longer, he'd decided not to wait.

With commercial transplantation prohibited in Australia, the United Kingdom and the United States, he'd sold his house and used the money to go overseas and purchase a black-market kidney from a country with a commercial programme giving donors a needed organ for monetary compensation. This alternative to waiting had proved to be a sometimes dangerous option for those who chose it, and it certainly seemed so for Lawrence.

Fergus shook the patient's hand. 'Good morning, Lawrence.'

The man was in his late twenties, dark-haired and unwell-looking. 'Hello again, Doc. Bet you didn't expect to see me again.'

'No. I'm sorry you're not well, old son.' Fergus turned to the team with a wry smile. 'Lawrence was over at Sydney East and decided to not wait for the donor programme. He went for broke — literally.'

He smiled at the young man and Ailee agreed with Fergus's non-judgemental attitude of Lawrence's choices.

Fergus turned to the staff. 'When Lawrence returned to Australia post-transplant he was well. Unfortunately, that didn't last. He's become concerned that his condition has deteriorated.'

He glanced down at the report in his hand. 'We've brought him in to fine-tune his medication regime, stabilise any damage if we can, and follow up a few of his concerns.'

He lowered his voice to speak directly to Lawrence. 'I've got your blood tests back and I'm afraid it is what you suspected. You contracted a blood-borne disease from your donor or the equipment during the procedure.'

Lawrence closed his eyes and sank back in the bed. 'You warned me.'

Fergus murmured to Ailee. 'Lawrence's condition has been complicated by contracting hepatitis B, despite his surgeon's assurance his donor had been screened. He'll need help with information and support so he can come to terms with that.'

Lawrence managed to smile wryly at Ailee. 'I suppose I can be glad it's not AIDS, but hepatitis B can be pretty rotten, too, can't it?'

Ailee felt her respect for the beleaguered young man rise at his attempt to be philosophical. 'Can be... or might not be.' She leaned towards him and touched his shoulder 'I'll have the communicable disease sister come and see you, Lawrence. Trudy can answer any questions and concerns that you have, as well as connect you to some support so you don't feel as isolated as you do now.'

Fergus nodded. 'When we sort out your medications, you'll feel better as well. Give yourself a few days to get over the shock and we'll have you as well as you can be before you leave.'

'Thanks, Doc.' Lawrence held out his hand. Fergus shook it and then rested his hand on the young man's shoulder for a moment before moving on.

Ailee saw the tension in the surgeon's shoulders, the slight bow of the usually lifted chin, and could tell that Fergus wasn't unaffected by Lawrence's plight.

Personal issues forgotten for the moment, she caught up to him and spoke quietly. 'It's a sad twist for him.'

Fergus turned his head to meet Ailee's eyes. 'It may be worse than a twist. Five of the last sixteen patients that I know of who have gone overseas have died within twelve months.'

Ailee said, 'If we could lift our donor rates, people like Lawrence wouldn't have to take this risk.'

They both knew contracting a blood-borne disease because of inadequate screening was one of the major causes of complications following commercial transplants.

His mouth compressed. 'The tragedy is that if we could lift our state donor rate to where it is in progressive places like,' he waved his hand, 'South Australia, even, Lawrence wouldn't have been driven to take the risks he had.'

Ailee nodded because she couldn't agree more. They desperately needed to raise public awareness for participation in the donor programme. Fergus felt as strongly as she did, that was not surprising but good, because donor promotion was dear to her heart.

Maurice came up to them and waited until Ailee looked at him in question. 'I wondered if you had time to explain haemodialysis again to Agnes, please, Ailee. I came to talk about her medications but she doesn't seem to understand dialysis and I know how good you are at explanations.'

Ailee was glad of the distraction because she was becoming more anxious about her reactions to Fergus. Her awareness. Her respect for him as a man. In fact, she'd skip the rest of the round because there was no further need for her here today.

And she needed to think. There was more here because her feelings were progressing to far more dangerous ground, seeing the way he dealt with his patients. His empathy. Hearing his passion for the donor program. This wasn't just about their Singapore stopover anymore. This was much, much more.

Ailee bit her lip and closed her eyes briefly. This was not the place to think about this.

She drew a deep breath and brushed her face as if to brush away non-work-related thoughts. There were a hundred things to do and she'd better get started.

The patient Maurice wanted her to see was an elderly lady who was almost – but not quite – at the dialysis stage and they'd met before.

When Ailee searched out Agnes, the white-haired woman's lined face still looked mapped with years of laughter. Just the sort of person Ailee needed. 'Hello again, Agnes. Maurice says you have some more questions about haemodialysis.'

'Haemo-whatever.' The old lady snorted. 'I suppose it would help if I could remember what to call the darned thing, but what I really want to know is how my blood can go into some machine dirty and come out clean without killing me.'

Ailee grinned. 'If it was my blood, I'd want to know, too.' She sat down beside Agnes. 'If you remember me saying, Agnes, with your increasing renal failure, the amount of water you are passing is getting less and less.'

'Hmmph,' said Agnes. 'And that's a good thing as I don't have to get up at night to pee, finally.'

Ailee shook her head. 'It will keep getting less until you might only pass an eggcup full of urine in twenty-four hours. That's not good.'

'Why not?' The older lady narrowed her eyes.

Ailee could tell Agnes was determined to understand this time. 'Because any extra fluids you swallow can't leave your body until the next three-times-a-week dialysis can remove it.'

'Oh.'

Oh, indeed. Ailee went on. 'Too much extra fluid in your bloodstream causes oedema, or water in your tissues – like swollen ankles – which puts a load on your heart. Your heart will blow up like a balloon to cope with the extra fluid and then deflate when dialysis takes the fluid off. All that stretching and deflating weakens your heart as well.'

Agnes nodded slowly. 'So, it's the fluid that's the problem?'

Ailee smiled. Agnes was catching on. 'Not just the fluid. Your kidneys are like a filter in a coffee-machine. They collect the impurities from your blood and send the wastes out in the urine. If your kidneys don't work, they won't filter and your body fills up with toxins.'

Agnes nodded and Ailee went on. 'The haemodialysis is your artificial kidney. You weigh yourself before being connected to the machine and your weight determines how much extra fluid needs to be removed while your blood is being cleaned.'

Agnes frowned. 'And if I don't have this haemo-whatever, I just die from the poisons and fluid that builds up in my body that I can't get rid of on my own?'

'Dialysis saves people's lives,' Ailee agreed, 'but still at best only provides fifteen per cent of what is called "normal" kidney function.'

'So I have to stay on the piddly amount of fluid I'm allowed to drink? Four cups, is it?'

'I'm afraid so. It can cause cramps if you drink too much and the machine has to take the extra out of your blood.'

'So how does the blood go in and out? Do they put a tap in or something?'

'Something like that,' Ailee said. 'Before you start treatment, one of our doctors will put a shunt in your arm—' Ailee pointed to a spot halfway between Agnes's hand and her elbow '—where they will connect you to the machine with a needle each time.'

Agnes rubbed her wrist and shuddered at the thought. 'So how does this coffee-machine clean my blood, or have you told me that bit and I didn't get it?'

'No, I'm slow but I'll get there.' The two women smiled at each other and Ailee went on. 'Dialysis is a lot to take in at one time and we'll go over it again at each stage.'

'Give me the good news,' Agnes snorted.

'Your blood is pumped through a plastic cylinder that contains thousands of very fine tubes. Each tube has tiny holes that let the waste and extra fluid pass through but not the blood cells or protein. A special fluid washes around the outside of the tubes so that your blood can be returned to you with the toxins removed.'

'So how long do I have to stay tied to the machine with a needle in my arm?'

'It takes about four hours for all your blood to pass through the machine about six times.'

'Blimey. And to think I never appreciated my kidneys.'

Ailee grinned. 'That's what I learnt when I came to work here.'

Agnes scratched her chin and the hair poking out under her lip wobbled. 'Okay, dearie. I'd say my old brain's done as well as it can.'

'Your brain is better than a lot of much younger people. It's a pretty heavy topic,' Ailee agreed, 'but each time you come in, ask more questions. Everyone is happy to help you understand what's happening. Good luck.'

Agnes had restored Ailee's sense of humour and she headed back to her office happier and without so much as glancing at Fergus as he completed the round. Unfortunately, she could still feel his gaze on the back of her neck all the way up the corridor.

The hours flew by but Ailee couldn't get the resignation in Lawrence's face out of her mind. The young man with the overseas transplant weighed on her. She supposed it was a mixed blessing as Lawrence distracted her from worrying about her appointment with Fergus later that day, but she wished she could help Lawrence.

As the clock crept around to five, Ailee put off her coming meeting with Fergus, and she dropped back to sit for a few minutes at the side of Lawrence's bed. 'How are you going, Lawrence?'

'I'm not too bad.' He looked at Ailee's handbag. 'Going home?'

'I am. Soon.'

'Mr McVicker said you're a doctor?'

'Yep. I'm Transplant Co-ordinator at the moment but I'm just filling in. How did you go with Trudy? Did she answer your questions about hepatitis B?'

Lawrence's eyes lit up. 'She's a special lady. You all are. She's coming back to see me again tomorrow.'

'That's great,' Ailee said.

'I thought everyone would think I was such a loser for going overseas and then being stupid enough to get burned.'

'We make decisions on what we think is good at the time. I'm sure your reasons were there.'

He raised his eyebrows comically but Ailee could see no humour in his sad blue eyes. 'Yeah. If I didn't go I wouldn't be here. Four years on dialysis wasn't for me.'

'I'm guessing it cramped your style?'

'That but worse.' He shrugged. 'I kept getting sick, and I couldn't handle being put on and off the donor programme.'

'Ah.' She understood that. 'Tough. That feeling of let down.' Her brother could have been this man in ten years.

He shook his head. 'I'd get depressed and have a few days on the booze and be even worse off.'

'Oh dear,' Ailee said. That happened too frequently, with young men especially.

'Yeah.' Lawrence scratched his head. 'When I came into dialysis I'd be way overloaded in fluid. The cramps would kill me when they had to draw off the extra fluid. I thought I'd speed the process up and go for a commercial kidney.'

Ailee said nothing for a moment then said, 'Others have done it and been lucky.'

'I wish I'd just done what Mr McVicker had said and waited.'

So did Ailee. She liked Lawrence.

He sighed. 'It was a gamble but I wouldn't have made the four years anyway.'

Ailee's gaze sharpened. 'It was that bad?' Just what did he mean?

He avoided her intent gaze. 'Not enough to live for.'

Oh, Lawrence. Where was his family? Ah, orphan she remembered. His friends? Ailee shook her head slowly. 'There's always enough to live for.'

His brows lifted. 'Spoken like a woman in charge of her life.' Lawrence smiled grimly. 'I don't have family, I can't work because I've been sick for two years, my friends feel bad when they're well and I'm not. It's not much fun and I don't see the point. I'm useless.'

Ailee disagreed. 'I don't see that. Everyone can make a difference. Lawrence, you have experiences that new end-stage kidney-disease sufferers could learn from. Promise me you'll give me a chance to help you help them.'

'You sound like Mr McVicker.' Lawrence mocked her. 'He was always going on about what I had to offer. I reckon I would have topped myself a year ago if it wasn't for Mr McVicker.'

'He's nagging you too.' Ailee refused to give up. 'That proves you're special. I have to go now, but I'll make a few enquiries, talk to some colleagues, and I'll see you tomorrow so we can talk some more. Okay?'

She rested her hand on his shoulder and left. She could feel the stinging in her throat for the sadness around Lawrence.

He didn't have a sister who would donate her kidney, and she wondered if she'd missed the times when William and all the other dialysis patients felt like Lawrence did. Depression could play such a large part in end-stage kidney disease and dialysis patients, and her new job was giving her time and space to talk more with clients than she'd ever had time for as a surgeon. What had started out as a favour for the ward had turned into a blessing in experience.

She was so absorbed in Lawrence's dilemma that she almost walked into Fergus. But she couldn't miss the man when he stood in front of her. Couldn't miss the swirl of his own special aftershave, the Fergus scent that she remembered, and the warmth of his body melding with hers despite the inches between them.

Ailee looked up and unexpectedly he smiled down into her face.

For a moment all she could do was bask in the gentleness in his eyes. She recognised that look and the way it made her feel. Something had changed between them today and suddenly she remembered why it was dangerous being around Fergus.

Rita came out of her office and Fergus raised his brows. She opened her mouth to say something, looked at them both and then suddenly, inexplicably, she turned around and walked away.

Ailee blinked. She'd been mooning and the warmth of embarrassment ran up her cheeks.

Time alone with Fergus was a very bad idea.

She'd forgotten the whole reason she'd backed away in Singapore.
Lawrence's situation should have reminded her like nothing else could
that some decisions were not good ones.

Fergus circled her elbow with his fingers and steered her towards
the door. 'Don't overthink it. Come with me before you change your
mind.'

Ailee found herself marching beside Fergus like a new army recruit.
Slowly her mind cleared and she realised what she was doing. She
stopped abruptly. 'Do you mind?'

She shook off his hand and rubbed her arm. She was awake now and
it was more important than ever to not become involved with Fergus.

'I thought you might have bolted,' he replied mildly.

'Was that an option?' she asked dryly. 'I'm only here because the air
needs clearing and I don't want this,' she waved her hand, 'railroading
that you seem to have decided on to happen again. You need to realise
that.'

Fergus ignored what Ailee had considered a good response under
pressure. 'I just want to talk. And talk when I can give you my full
attention,' was all he said.

He stopped beside a bottle-green Jaguar, long and sleek with a waft
of warm new leather puffing out with the air when he opened the door
for her. He waited for her to enter. At least he didn't try manhandling
her into the seat.

She narrowed her eyes at him and wondered if she might just say
she'd changed her mind. He stared back, something in his face said
he would follow if she walked away – and that they had to have this
conversation sometime. She glared at him and eased into the luxurious

car, sinking into the soft leather seat. For now, she'd have to accept her escape wasn't in his plans, but that would be his only win.

Capitulation wasn't in her plans. He'd find that out. Soon.

Ailee sat and he closed the door with a satisfied slam. She clenched her fingers and then carefully straightened her fingers so he wouldn't see. She was darned if she'd let him know he put her on edge.

Fergus glanced at her before he started the car. 'Thank you for coming.'

Fat lot of choice. She lifted her chin. 'Where are we going?'

'You don't want to be alone. I want to be private. So, we're going to my house. My housekeeper and her husband are there.'

'And your daughter?'

'Simone won't be home for several hours. She has a self-defence class this afternoon.'

Ailee laughed without mirth. 'I need self-defence to stop people forcing me into cars against my will.'

His lips twitched and she realised she hadn't seen him smile much since Singapore. 'I didn't force you, I just leant in a little.'

'Semantics.'

He looked across at her as he started the car. 'I'll take you home any time you ask.'

She opened her mouth, but before she could speak he added quickly to qualify his statement. 'As soon as we've had our talk.'

Ailee closed her mouth again, but strangely she did believe his promise. It should have reassured her. Naturally, it didn't.

They lapsed into silence during the short drive, silent until they passed through remote-controlled gates, Ailee remembering she'd met this man in business class on an aircraft and that he came from a different world to her. The established gardens were green and luscious.

The imposing white-columned building nestled like a shell surrounded by manicured lawns and a high stone wall that prevented those on the outside from looking in. 'You have a beautiful home.' She guessed such wealth showed his commitment to and passion for his job, because he surely didn't need to work for the money.

'It was my mother's house, and before you ask, yes, I did have a mother.'

'Would I say that?' Suddenly she felt lighter, calmer and at ease with him. Maybe it was just because they were away from the hospital, but the warmth in his eyes told her he could feel it, too.

He smiled. 'You would say anything if I made you wild enough.'

Ailee tossed her hair. 'I don't get that wild.'

His eyes darkened and though he didn't say it, it was as if he'd whispered, *I've seen you wild*.

Suddenly their laughter disappeared and the silence in the car felt like a wind tunnel that sucked away Ailee's breath and strength until she felt she could barely lift her head.

Fergus dragged in his own breath and tore his eyes from her face. 'Thank you for coming,' he said.

He climbed out, walked round the car then opened her door, and she accepted his help, powerless to resist. Fergus rested his fingers on her arm as she stood. He didn't say anything as they walked towards the front door but his touch on her burned and her surroundings faded.

An elderly woman in an apron, with a creased face and red cheeks opened the door with a welcoming, 'Hello, come in.' Bright eyes sparkled with delight.

Ailee smiled. Couldn't help it.

'This is my housekeeper, Martha. Martha, Dr Ailee Green.'

Martha and Ailee shook hands briefly.

Ailee said, 'Fergus mentioned you and your husband.'

'Aye. And he's mentioned you, too,' Martha responded. 'I've put tea in the library, Fergus. Ring if you want me.'

'We'll be there in a moment.' Fergus ignored the lift of Martha's brows as he steered Ailee across the black and white tiled entry and past an open carved wooden door.

Ailee looked into the room as they went by and saw a round table with cups, a teapot and a basket of tiny cakes.

'Was that the library?' Ailee craned her neck.

'Yes.' But his hand moved to the small of her back as they arrived at the bottom of the stairs. 'I'd like to show you something first. Please.'

Could she? Could she trust herself? Ailee had the first flutter of panic as they ascended and Fergus didn't look at her as they reached the next floor.

'We'll have tea in a moment. I promise.' He stopped in front of another closed door and turned the handle, indicating she should precede him into the room.

A moment... They'd have tea in a moment. She swallowed and tried to settle her heart rate with that tiny reassurance — surely not a lot could happen in a mere moment?

This room was a bedroom, though not your usual bedroom, more of a 1920s showcase and a window into the past.

The enormous four-poster bed was austere in maroon and gold covers, softened by a mound of cushions. A dressing-table shone with polish and several mirrors and a tapestry-seated chest gleamed in the corner. The room didn't look lived in. And it obviously wasn't his room. That had to be good. Didn't it?

But they'd be alone. In a bedroom. She looked up at him and suddenly imagined the exact sensations of a rabbit caught in headlights.

Fergus paused at the alarm in her face, said, 'Trust me,' as he crossed the room and hesitated. 'Just a little experiment.' He stopped and in slow motion he pulled her gently in front of him until her back was firm against his chest so that they both faced towards the mirror.

She could see their reflections in the glass.

Her body was framed by his, her spine rigid and unbending against him, and her eyes and mouth were narrow with wariness.

'That's one picture,' he said enigmatically. His eyes met hers in the mirror and she saw his intention before he moved, slowly, not to startle her and she realised the kiss was as inevitable as his hand turning her body to face him.

She stood there, captive, and his beautiful eyes darkened to black and melted her resistance with barely any effort.

'Ailee,' he whispered, her name a part of the kiss as his lips descended. Her eyelashes fluttered closed and she could do nothing but savour the homecoming of his mouth against her own bending to meet him.

His lips were softness and warmth giving way to the slow build-up of heat and firmness, growing more demanding and finally plundering until her hands clutched at his neck, seeking purchase in the storm, and then she demanded right back.

A slaking, satisfying, quenching kiss that she hadn't realised she'd needed but once started couldn't get enough of, and his arms held her safely away from the intrusion of the world into this timeless interlude her body needed but her brain denied.

Finally, a few minutes or many minutes later, achingly slowly, he drew away and his hands held her shoulders until her legs regained their strength.

She opened her eyes as he turned them to face the mirror again and a different woman stood there.

This woman was flushed, her languorous eyes complemented red swollen lips and she leant back against him for much-needed support. Breathless and disorientated, her breasts ached and the fire in her belly throbbed in time to her heartbeat. She shook her head to deny they could share all that with one kiss.

He lifted her hand and kissed the inside of her wrist before gently leading her across the room. 'That explains a lot of things, don't you think? Perhaps we'd better move on before it gets out of hand. This way.'

Still holding her fingers he drew her past the bed and opened another door. 'You can freshen up in here. I'll meet you in the library when you're ready.'

Ailee nodded, still stunned and with the tiniest gleam of something else. Annoyance? Or was it frustration? Disappointment?

She heard him leave and she sank down onto a stool in the ornate bathroom, rested her head back against the cold tiled wall and closed her eyes.

It felt as if she'd climbed a cliff and jumped off rather than a flight of stairs and been kissed in a room. She wondered if he'd known it was going to be like that, how long he'd planned to do that, and if he was amused or perhaps as frustrated as she was.

Whatever. She needed to explain her reasons, tell him about William, make Fergus realise he had to walk away before they got in any deeper, until she was free to live her own life.

A few minutes later, Ailee entered the library and she avoided his eyes. Instead, she looked at the portrait above the mantelpiece, the figure in the frame dominated the room.

'My mother,' Fergus said, but Ailee didn't need to be told that.

The woman was tall, judging by the rail on the staircase she stood beside. Her hair, the same chocolate brown as Fergus's, was coiled in a knot at her neck and the dark bedroom eyes were eerily similar to the ones Ailee had had no defence against barely ten minutes ago.

'She was a beautiful woman.'

Fergus nodded. 'Simone takes after her.'

Ailee half smiled. 'So does her son.'

She looked away from the compelling portrait and raised her chin. 'You shouldn't have brought me here, Fergus.'

'That's the first time you've called me Fergus since you left my bed.'

After what had happened upstairs she'd known it was on his mind, but she hadn't expected him to be so brazen about it. His words struck low in her stomach and she sucked in her breath. 'Don't.'

'Don't what?' He narrowed his eyes like a hunter sensing prey, and she lifted her chin. Back off buddy. She turned her back on him, as if she didn't consider him a danger, and walked to the window that looked out over the lawn. 'Don't remind me. Singapore was a mistake and I need to explain why.'

He ignored the latter half of her sentence and concentrated on one word. 'And what just happened, or nearly happened upstairs... was that a mistake, too?' He raised his eyebrows, daring her to dispute the truth. 'I've never felt anything less mistaken. We connected... *we connect*. The same happened in Singapore and then you left. With that ridiculous note, as if we'd shared a cup of tea.'

She glanced back at him and the sombre note in his voice made her frown.

He stroked the lid of the steaming pot Martha had left and then crossed the room to stand beside her shoulder, not touching – as if he couldn't trust himself – but close enough for her to feel his heat.

She turned her face away and he went on.

'Why did you leave like that? You agreed we should see each other in Sydney. I didn't dream that connection, Ailee. Did I?'

He reached out with one long, elegant finger and lifted her chin until she was forced to look at him.

This was a disaster. She should never have come. This was one hundred per cent his battleground and she needed to get out of there. 'Yes, there was a connection, but I need air. Take me outside. I need to explain but I can't breathe in here.'

His eyes glittered and he gestured with a hand at a doorway. 'You're probably right. Walking away from you upstairs was one of the hardest things I've ever done.'

Oh great. They were both having control issues. Not what she wanted to hear. 'Well, you're larger than life in this room, too.' And she wasn't sure what would happen if he kissed her again. Something must have shown in her face because as she watched his eyes darkened again.

Oh, Fergus. You could make me do things I'd never dream of doing, things that would go against my own moral compass. She didn't say it out loud; it was bad enough admitting it to herself.

'You're right. We'll go outside, I will give you some space, but I want answers.'

Which she'd been trying to give him.

He led the way to a side door into a conservatory furnished with white cane furniture and dozens of lush green potted plants. In another time and place she would have loved this room. The windows were full-length French doors and he opened one to allow her to precede him onto the tiled balcony.

She drew a deep breath at the fresh air – and the space she quickly made between them – and headed for the stone steps that connected the balcony to the lawn.

Fergus caught up with her on the grass, but stayed hands off. As promised. 'I think I had it right the first time. We did connect. Yet when you left like that, I assumed you didn't care. Was I wrong? If you tell me you didn't feel the same, I'll leave you alone and never speak of it again.' His eyes bored into hers, dark and compelling, daring her to give him the truth. They narrowed as she hesitated. 'Don't lie to me, Ailee.'

It would be so easy. Just lie and say he meant nothing to her. Ailee opened her mouth and then closed it again. She couldn't. She had to be honest with him.

'Yes. You're right. There is something between us.' She paused. 'But...'

She felt him stiffen beside her, but she raised a hand in case he was thinking of interrupting. 'The time of our meeting couldn't have been worse,' she went on. 'What I see in you is something I've waited a long time to find, but Singapore wasn't the time.'

Fergus shook his head. 'What about now? I know I'm moving fast. Hell, we both move faster than light when we're together, but I can't let you get away now that I've found you.'

He was right beside her now and slid his hand possessively over the curve of her shoulder until her skin glowed with heat from his hand.

'For goodness sake, if you're not going to listen I'm leaving.' His hand fell to his side and she lifted her chin.

'You tremble when I touch you.' His face twisted into a cynical smile. 'What do you think that means?'

He went on. 'I've seen too much of life not to know my mind. I thought about how complicated you were going to make my world the first time I saw you.'

She felt the tears stinging at the backs of her eyes and she blinked them away. This was too important. Yes, she could destroy this beautiful man if something unexpected happened during her operation or afterwards.

'That's exactly why this is such poor timing. I don't need this pressure. There is so much going on in my life at this moment that you don't know about. You and your daughter don't need someone you can't trust not to be there in your life.'

He looked at her and for the first time she felt he really listened. Thank goodness.

'Not be there in what way?' His words glided between them like a cool breeze, zephyr-like yet sharp. 'And we'll leave my daughter out of this.'

'Your daughter is part of the reason.'

And then Simone was there. The dark-haired young girl dressed in a martial arts kit ran across the lawn to meet them. 'Hello. I'm home. Who's your friend?'

Simone McVicker was a miniature of the woman in the portrait and obviously another determined lady.

Fergus turned slowly and faced his daughter. 'Hello, Simone. What happened to martial arts?'

'Chrissy Smythe fell and broke her wrist and Mr Ting had to go with her to the hospital so we finished early.'

Fergus nodded. 'Poor Chrissy.' He turned to Ailee. 'Dr Ailee Green, meet my daughter, Simone.'

Ailee held out her hand and shook the girl's fingers, which flopped like a wilted flower. Ailee tried to contain the twitch of her lips. Simone was playing droopy princess, and suppressing her amusement was a struggle.

Simone looked Ailee up and down as they held hands. 'You're very tall, aren't you? I'm going to be tall like my father and grandmother.'

Ailee smiled. 'Yes, I can see that. But you shake hands like a fish.'

The young girl blinked, stared, tightened her grip and shook hands properly.

Slowly they smiled at each other.

'Do you work with my dad at the new hospital?'

Ailee nodded. 'I'm one of the transplant co-ordinators at the moment.'

'Can you do operations?'

Ailee nodded. 'I've just finished three months in Scotland with a professor in renal surgery.'

She saw his eyes widen as Fergus stared at her. 'Professor Giles? At the Edinburgh Infirmary?'

'And Ian Forrest. But enough of me. I'd really like a cup of tea and one of those gorgeous-looking cakes that Martha has waiting in the library.'

Simone clapped her hand over her mouth. 'I was supposed to remind you of that. We'd better go in.'

They all turned and headed for the house and Ailee felt surprised by how far they'd walked. Probably because she'd been walking quickly to escape the impending disclosures that she still hadn't made. As if the universe was conspiring – or Simone's friend's wrist.

Now his daughter was involved. Had met her. It would make it harder not to upset them.

Fergus stayed silent and she wondered if he regretted taking her upstairs to kiss her instead of hearing her reasons for fobbing him off. Served him right.

For the next half hour there was no chance for Fergus to ask anything because his daughter monopolised Ailee's attention as if she were starved of female conversation.

Simone could talk while she poured, though, and Ailee couldn't help being impressed with her hostess skills.

'So, who do you think has the best dress sense?' Simone pointed to a magazine with two glamorous young women on the cover as a plate of dainty cakes changed hands.

Ailee looked at Fergus for help and he shook his head with a small smile on his face. 'Um... they're singers,' he clarified, obviously trying hard to stay up to scratch with his daughter's favourites.

'Definitely her. I like the paisley dress and the boots.' Ailee didn't know the other one but she'd look out for her. She took a bite and the morsel melted in her mouth.

Simone was too busy talking to eat. 'Do you ski? My father promised me a holiday skiing but then chose to work during his holidays.' She pouted.

Ailee glanced at Fergus, who said nothing in his own defence. 'Not quite a choice. I know three young people whose lives have been drastically changed because your dad came when our hospital needed him. One of them could have died if we hadn't found a replacement surgeon.' She softened her words with a smile. 'It is disappointing for you, though.'

Simone looked at her father and she narrowed her gaze thoughtfully. 'Okay. But I have compensation coming my way and I'd really like to go to New Zealand in the winter. Except he hates planes.'

Ailee remembered that Fergus had said she'd helped his phobia. Those memories made her remember other things. Luckily Simone prattled on. 'They say New Zealand's even better than Thredbo.'

Ailee was having trouble keeping up because every subject seemed to bring back more memories that she'd locked away from that time with Fergus. 'Sorry. Haven't tried skiing but I have been to New Zealand and it is lovely.'

'I had a friend from New Zealand in my dorm. I was a boarder at school but Dad said he missed me too much, so I came home. I don't believe him—' a glance at her dad, '—but I like being a day student better.'

Fergus met Ailee's amused glance and tilted his head in acknowledgment.

Well, well. She was glad he'd decided to bring his daughter home. Simone seemed a bright young woman, if a little hard on Fergus, but they'd had a tough couple of years.

Simone tilted her head at Ailee after refilling her father's tea. 'Are you staying for dinner?'

'No.' Ailee put down her empty plate. 'I promised my mother I'd be home for a family dinner, which I hope I can still eat after all those cakes. I should go; it's getting late.'

They all stood. Simone hadn't taken her eyes off Ailee. 'Will you come and visit again?'

'We'll see. But it has been lovely to meet you, Simone.' Ailee held out her hand, sure that this time the grip would be a normal one.

Simone ignored her hand, hugged Ailee, and then kissed her cheek.

'I liked meeting you, too. Dad never brings women home.'

'I'm honoured.' Ailee looked at Fergus and dreaded the trip in the car. Suddenly she couldn't face the whole explanation scene and her nerves felt shattered. 'Would you like me to order a taxi, Fergus? It would save you going out again.'

'I'll drive you home.' There was no doubt that Fergus had earmarked the return journey for some information-sharing and Ailee felt even more like a moth in a web.

'Can I come?' Simone's request hung in the air and Ailee avoided Fergus as she looked at his daughter. 'I don't mind, but it's up to your father.'

Simone didn't look at Fergus either. 'The only problem is I get sick in the back.'

Even better. Ailee was quick to offer. 'I'll sit in the back, and you can sit with your father in the front.'

'No, you won't.' Fergus said it mildly enough but there was an implacable note that both women knew meant not negotiable.

Simone studied her father. 'I could probably sit in the back for a short trip,' she suggested, and as they moved towards the door she whispered to Ailee, 'You wanted me to come, didn't you?'

'Thanks,' Ailee said and Simone gave a satisfied nod.

The car journey passed with strain, the whole afternoon to explain had been a fiasco and exercise in frustration and when Fergus opened her door back at the hospital, his words brushed her neck as she climbed out.

'My fault. We should have talked first. I'll ring you.' Then he helped his daughter into the front and walked back to his own door.

'Thank you for the tea and cakes,' Ailee said politely.

There was humour in the look Fergus gave her. 'It was an interesting afternoon. I'll speak to you soon.'

Chapter 14

Fergus

Fergus watched Ailee in the rear-view mirror as he drove away, noting she didn't turn around to wave. Serve him right. He'd blown that.

She'd told him, in actual words, that he was the man she was looking for but "the timing was off". What did that mean?

As he drove, he mulled over what could possibly be Ailee's reasons for holding back?

He decided it could be she had a tortured past and had been hurt by some man. He could deal with that. These were all things he'd never thought to have to consider again, since he'd never intended re-entering the awkward mating game after his wife had died.

He admitted to himself that he was back where he'd been in Singapore after they'd shared the day together. Thinking long term, beyond to life and marriage, with Ailee as Simone's step-mother.

To his intense surprise he wasn't fazed by any of those long-term concepts, only that the plan could fail if Ailee continued to oppose his suit for her "reasons". Would a time come when the reasons would go away? He'd almost found out today. Except Simone had intervened.

And met Ailee. And was drawn to her. Which he'd been hoping to avoid in case it all came to nothing, now there would be some personal cost. But he was willing to take that risk. He had to be careful, though, for Simone's sake.

'You like her, don't you, Dad?'

He'd thought Simone had been listening to her earpods, which travelled everywhere with her. He glanced across at his daughter. The expression on her face reminded him of her mother when she'd been indulgent of his "man's" ways.

The usual pain from his loss of Stella didn't come as viciously these days — had moved to wonderful memories and reminiscences – and for this he was thankful.

He smiled at the tiny warming from his daughter. It was unusual for Simone to initiate a conversation except today with Ailee, he thought wryly. 'Yes, I do, Simone. I think you like her, too.' He slowed the car as he looked across at his daughter again.

'I think she's neat and I think she's kind, too. Elizabeth Arrow's stepmother is a witch.'

He suppressed a laugh. Just. 'I don't think Ailee would be a witch.'

'Nope. And she's a surgeon like you.'

One of the issues.

Simone said conversationally, 'It would be good for you to have another woman around for a change. You might stay home more... especially if she has a baby.'

Fergus nearly ran into the gate as he drove into his driveway. His daughter was way ahead of him.

'I might need to get to know Ailee better before we start contemplating babies,' he said dryly. 'And I'd really prefer if you didn't mention this conversation to anyone at school. Okay?' Or to Ailee if his daughter met her again. Which she would if he had anything to say about it.

'Sure, Dad. And you should take it slowly. You don't want to scare her off.'

His daughter was twelve going on twenty and it was darned scary.

Chapter 15

Ailee

Ailee heard the car pull away and forced herself not to turn around. She wanted to stamp her foot. Looked up at the sky and felt like shaking her fist. 'Darn it. He should've known by now.' It should all have been out and sorted. The longer she left it the bigger her secret loomed, which was ridiculous. Of all the people in the world to understand, Fergus should.

But there was his daughter. Whom she'd now met. And liked.

Still, she needed to think through the implications of the last hour, of Fergus at least knowing it was the timing of their "connection" not him she was fighting.

She had the weekend to get it right before Monday. Ailee glanced at her watch and her eyes widened. She had only enough time to jump in her car and make it home before her mother's roast was ruined.

'So how was work?' William appeared quite chirpy at the dinner table. He'd only just come in from being out with some friends and looked different to his usual solemn self.

'Work was fine.' Ailee glanced at his plate. 'And since when do you eat bananas?'

Ailee raised her eyebrows at the tiny half-banana William had tucked under his plate and, caught out, her brother shrugged.

'It's my once-a-month treat, and I'm having dialysis tomorrow.'

William knew he had to be careful of foods that contained "dangerous salts" like potassium, and his fluid restrictions were the part he hated the most. When he was well enough, he went out with his friends on Friday nights. He couldn't drink alcohol, mainly because of the fluid amounts involved and the chemicals his body couldn't get rid of.

Like most dialysis patients, William had established a good rapport with the staff and the mostly older patients who came into the dialysis clinic at the hospital on the same days as he did. Unlike less fortunate end-stage kidney-disease sufferers, William knew it was ending soon. He was guaranteed a kidney. Hers.

Ailee smiled across at her brother. 'You're looking stronger.'

'I'm getting there. The next assessment clinic will be the big test and it's not far off. I'm pretty nervous about that.'

Ailee put down her knife and fork. Showed her hands. 'I've got my fingers crossed.'

Helen looked across at her son because she knew how much depended on it. 'William said the man standing in for Mr Harry seems very good. Do you think he'll be the one who does the surgery if it all goes ahead quickly?'

Ailee hadn't considered that. It was a disquieting thought and she wasn't so sure Fergus would be happy either when he found out who the donor was. But she'd get there before then. Though, the way it was going he'd find out in theatre. She almost laughed at that. Because that would not happen!

She concentrated on her mother's question to avoid thinking about Fergus operating on William. 'Fergus McVicker has been seconded from Sydney East. It all depends on Mrs Harry and how quickly she recovers from her stroke whether Mr McVicker stays on for two or four weeks.'

Her mother still looked worried at the change of surgeon at this late stage, so Ailee went on, when the last thing she wanted to do – which was talk about Fergus. 'He's dedicated and a whiz in theatre. It seems that he's the best laparoscopic surgeon in Australia.'

'Then William can't lose, whoever the surgeon is. We need the best when my only two children depend on the team.' Helen put her napkin to her lips and closed her eyes. Then she smiled tremulously and stood up. 'I'll just get some more vegetables,' she said brightly, and left the table.

William and Ailee looked at each other and Ailee stood. They both knew their mother would be crying in the kitchen and Ailee touched her brother's shoulder as she followed her mother.

Helen wiped her eyes as her daughter came in. 'We'll be fine,' Ailee said.

'I know. I'm being a drama queen.'

Ailee smiled and dropped a kiss on her mother's cheek. 'No, you're not. You're being a wonderful, caring mother and we wouldn't have you any other way.'

Later that evening, Ailee searched out William after her mother had gone to bed. She leaned over his chair and ruffled his hair. 'Hey, Will. How's it going?'

William smiled crookedly up at her and shrugged. 'The usual.'

Ailee sat down next to him. 'Do you mind if I ask you something?'

'Shoot.'

'How are you coping with dialysis? I know you hate it and I know you don't have much choice, but it must be hard, especially when you're going through a rough patch like the last couple of weeks.'

William's eyes slid away. 'Dialysis sucks but death is worse. I guess that keeps me going.'

Such basic equations from an eighteen-year-old made Ailee wince. He shrugged and began to scroll through his phone. Not looking at her. Ailee thanked God that her brother still felt it was worth it.

After talking to Lawrence — had it only been today? — she'd been worried William was becoming morbid, too. She'd noticed a few deviations from his usual happy self and even wondered if they'd lost a little closeness since she'd come home.

'Come on, Will. Talk to me. What's going on in that clever head of yours?'

William fiddled with his phone. Gave a heavy sigh. 'Dialysis keeps me alive. But it's a pain. Three days a week, at least, tied to a machine for half the day. Watching everything you eat. Can't go out with my mates and have a few drinks. This horrible fistula—' he shook his wrist where his veins stood out, scarred and bulging where a grafted artery had strengthened his vein for needle access to his bloodstream '—would scare any self-respecting girl away. They'd probably think I'm a drug addict anyway because of the needle marks up my arm.'

'Oh, Will.'

He held up a hand. Pushing her sympathy away. Curled his mouth up. 'The day before I go for dialysis, I feel sick because my blood's filling up with toxins. The day after treatment I need to recover from the strain of the procedure and the cramps 'cos they have to take extra fluid off. I can't remember when I last felt really well.' He sniffed. 'They tell me all that will change after the op, but the drug regime to stop your kidney being rejected seems pretty heavy. I'm not hanging out for that either.'

Poor Will. 'I can't imagine from your side. It must feel never ending.' Ailee nodded. 'We're here for you. I think you're incredibly brave.'

He shrugged and then looked away. 'We all know you're the brave one.'

She couldn't see his eyes or his expression. For a moment Ailee thought there was a bitter note to her brother's voice, but then he smiled up at her and she pushed the feeling away. But a tendril of disquiet made her belly hurt.

On Saturday morning Ailee woke in her lonely bed, and as her dreams faded, she thought of Fergus and the way he'd kissed her yesterday. In the dream his arms had been around her, the warmth and scent and feel of him so close, and she thought back to the way he'd looked with his fingers stroking her body, and she wanted those things again.

But if she wanted those things, she would have to include him in her plans, and her reasons for not doing so remained the same.

Ailee rolled over and pulled the pillow over her head to block out the bright light. She'd slept late because it had taken her so long to get to sleep after that worrying conversation with her brother.

Her phone rang and Ailee scrambled out of bed to disconnect it from the charger before it woke William. She wasn't on call as co-ordinator so it wouldn't be work. 'Hello?'

'Ailee?' She recognised Fergus's voice immediately and her grip tightened.

'Fergus.' She glanced to the bedroom door and checked it was shut. 'Did I wake you?'

There was amusement in Fergus's voice and she couldn't help the curve of her own lips. 'Yes. For some reason it took me ages to get to sleep.'

'Neither could I. But it's Saturday.'

'So?'

'Simone likes tennis and we have a court here. I suggested she have some friends around and she asked if you would come, too. Any chance?'

'I'm not very good with a tennis racket.' It was a lame excuse and nowhere near the definite no she'd meant to say.

'There's three other pre-adolescent females coming. I'll be out-numbered. Help.'

'I'm sure you'll manage,' she responded, but she couldn't keep the smile from her voice. Imagining big, fearless Fergus brought undone by a gaggle of adolescent females.

'They're already here. And I'm not. How about I pick you up in an hour?'

He was railroading her again. She really needed to put a stop to that. But, on the other hand, this might provide a new opportunity to finish her interrupted explanation of why she couldn't start a relationship with him. 'You don't know where I live.'

'My next question.'

'No. I'll drive myself.' And then I can bring myself home when I want to, she thought. Especially after I tell him about William, I might need that escape.

'If you insist.' There was a small pause. 'See you soon, then.'

Ailee climbed out of bed and wandered down the hallway. 'Was that you on the phone, darling?' Helen was on her way to the kitchen.

'Someone from work, inviting me for a game of tennis.'

'I hope you said yes.'

Ailee looked at her mother and then she laughed. 'Yes, Mother. I will go out and play.'

Helen smiled sheepishly. 'Well, since you got home from Scotland you haven't left our sides except to go to work. You need to have your own life, especially while you're well enough.'

Ailee hugged her mother. 'I'll be well after this operation, too, so stop worrying.'

When she arrived at the McVicker house, there was a red sports car and a long saloon parked outside the front door. Two curvy blonde women sailed down the front stairs past Ailee and shook their heads.

'Better him than us,' one of them said. She looked Ailee up and down and then smiled. 'If you're looking for a wild time, it's happening in there.'

Ailee smiled bemusedly at the women and climbed
the stairs.

A slightly fazed Martha opened the door and ushered her in warmly. 'Now, you might be able to sort this, Dr Green. I fear Fergus is out of his depth. In the library.'

Loud music pounded from speakers shaking the windows. She couldn't remember speakers in the book-lined room.

She walked across and opened the library door, and the music assaulted her ears, along with the visual impact of four short-skirted pre-teens in crop tops, short shorts and tennis shoes gyrating to the rhythm.

At first, she couldn't see Fergus but then spotted him peering at a mobile phone, obviously searching for the volume control. Simone grinned and waved as Ailee dodged past the dancers with a little gyration of her own until she came up behind Fergus.

'It's here,' Ailee shouted, but it was her finger, not her voice, that drew his attention, as she slid the volume control down to barely painful.

As she did so, she turned to catch Simone's eye and tapped her ears to explain the change in volume. Simone shrugged and nodded but seemed happy enough.

Ailee pointed to the connecting door to the observatory and Fergus agreed with fervour.

The door shut out almost half of the sound but obviously that wasn't enough for him. He took Ailee's hand and steered her to the outside terrace, and when that door was shut as well it was almost peaceful in the warm outside air.

'Good grief. Thank you for coming.' He gestured to a white wrought-iron table and chairs and waited until she was seated under the shade of an open umbrella before he sat.

As if by magic, Martha appeared as with orange juice and ice cubes in tall glasses for them and a jug and smaller glasses for the invaders when they came.

'Much more sensible outside, I agree, Dr Green.'

'Please, call me Ailee, Martha, and thank you for this.' She gestured to her glass.

'I see it's a little quieter now,' Martha teased Fergus. He took it good-naturedly as his housekeeper left them.

Ailee laughed. 'You shouldn't have bought Simone such big speakers.'

Fergus held up his hands and waved then. 'Not my fault. One of the little darlings brought it with her this morning.'

'What an enterprising female. Why so deafening?'

'Apparently that was Simone's all-time favourite song and it needs to be "Immersive Sound" to be really appreciated.'

'I was immersed. You were drowning.'

'Thank you, dear life raft.' His admiring gaze ran over her T-shirt and long shorts then back to her face. 'You look gorgeous.'

'Thank you, kind sir. I don't own a tennis skirt. You don't look bad yourself.' Fergus lounged in cargo shorts and an open-necked white shirt and they smiled at each other in mutual admiration and a sigh into their quiet space.

It didn't last long. The peace shattered as the girls poured through the conservatory door and circled their table.

'Hello, Ailee.' Simone grinned. 'Have you come to save Dad from us?'

'How did you guess?' Ailee grinned right back. 'So, who have we here?'

'Demi, Peyton, and Ava.' Simone pointed out each girl — one with braces, one with bright red nail polish, and one with the sweetest face and smile.

Mentally, Ailee dubbed them dentist, polish, and angel so that she would remember their names.

'Demi, Peyton and Ava.' The names matched the prompts and she had them in her memory now. 'How do you do?'

Chapter 16

Fergus

After refreshments they all trooped towards the tennis court and Fergus watched his daughter hang back to walk with Ailee.

Simone seemed shy for a second, which sat strangely after the noise with her friends, and made him hope he was doing the right thing by encouraging this friendship.

'Thanks for coming, Ailee,' he heard Simone say.

'Thank you for the invitation.' She glanced conspiratorially at the young girl. 'I wouldn't have missed your father with his hands over his ears. All we need to do now is beat him at tennis and I can go home happy.'

Simone glanced across at him with a smile and Fergus savoured the laughter on both their faces and the fact that he was included in his daughter's warmth.

'I may give you a run for your money,' he said mildly as he put the racket bag he was carrying down on the bench beside the court.

'You girls have a game first and we'll watch and then Ailee and I will play the losers.'

The morning passed with much hilarity, especially when Ailee teased Fergus about his poor level of play.

They'd swapped the teams around several times and Ailee and Simone were now playing against Fergus and Peyton.

'We win,' Ailee crowed, as they met at the net to shake hands. She grinned widely at Fergus and he smiled down at her.

'Will we tell her?' he asked his daughter.

Simone's eyes sparkled with laughter as she broke their secret to Ailee. 'Dad's been playing with his left hand all morning and he's right-handed.'

'That's terrible. Here I was thinking I wasn't too bad at all. I won't have it. Play with your right hand and don't hold back, Fergus McVicker.'

One more game later, Ailee and Simone walked off without having scored a point and now the other girls wanted to play Fergus with his right hand. Simone and Ailee sat down beside one of Martha's jugs of iced orange and sparkling water as Ailee pretended to be offended. 'He's too good.'

Simone smiled across at her father, who had easily lobbed a shot back to the far corner of the court to have his opponents scrambling. 'He's been hilarious today. My friends said he was a crack-up.' She looked a little surprised to be proud of him.

'Hmm,' Ailee said, mock seriously. 'His sense of humour is a wonderful part of him. Along with his rotten left-handed tennis skills.'

Simone smiled and then her expression turned more serious. 'We haven't used the court together since my mum died.'

'I'm sorry about your mum. Your dad misses her too. You should play together more often. I know he misses being your friend.' She tested Simone's reaction to talking about Stella's death. 'Your father said it was a shock to everyone when your mother had complications after surgery.'

Simone stared across the grass. 'It should never have happened. How can a doctor not be able to save his own wife? How could Dad let it happen?'

Ailee slipped her arm around Simone's shoulders and hugged her before sitting back. 'Anger is a part of grief but maybe it's hurting you now. Your dad is a very talented surgeon, but I guess they wouldn't have let him anywhere near your mother. Surgeons aren't allowed to operate on or look after their own family.'

Simone looked at Ailee. 'Has anyone died while you were operating?'

'No, but sometimes I've had to operate on people who have just died so they can donate their organs to others.'

Simone shook her head as if to ward off the mental picture. 'I don't want to think about that or that part of my dad's work.'

'Okay.' Ailee raised her eyebrows. 'But transplants are a big part and he's one of the leaders in Australia. Lots of patients think he's a hero.'

Ailee refilled both their glasses before continuing. 'Tell me about when you boarded at school. Is it better as a day student now?'

'Heaps better. Actually—' she looked across at her father '—I think it made me appreciate Dad more. I missed him when I stayed away all week, even though he's not here much.'

Ailee smiled. 'I think he missed you, too.'

'He must have.' Simone glanced across at her father, who was shaking hands at the net with her friends. 'He asked if I'd rather come home again.'

The others joined them.

Fergus poured himself a drink and raised it to his daughter. 'Great game, Simone. I'm most impressed.' Simone glowed with the praise and Fergus put the empty glass down and rubbed her back with affection.

Pleasure warmed inside her to see Simone lean back into her father and smile up at him. If there had been a rift then things were definitely getting better there. Fergus met Ailee's eyes over the top of his daughter's dark hair and he looked the most relaxed she'd seen him. Except for the time that he'd slept by her side and she'd crept away.

She pushed that thought away. Any positive results for Fergus's relationship with his daughter made her visit worthwhile – but dangerous. Ailee would leave soon, let them have some time together when the others went home. There wasn't going to be an opportunity to discuss William today. Her difficult discussion would have to wait.

'Let's go up and have lunch.' Fergus rounded up the rackets and repacked the bag, while Ailee and the girls collected the glasses. They all trooped up to the house where Martha had sandwiches and savoury pies ready to serve.

The other girls left soon after lunch, and Ailee glanced at her watch.

'I might head off, too.'

Fergus looked up with a frown and Simone pouted.

Ailee smiled at Simone. 'Have some time with your dad. He doesn't get you to himself very much and you have all afternoon. I have to do some things at home.'

'Will you come back another time?'

'Absolutely.' She pretended to scowl at Fergus. 'Right after I have tennis lessons.'

Simone laughed at the tennis reference and they walked Ailee out to her car. Simone hugged Ailee and Ailee encircled the young girl's slim form and hugged her back. 'Thanks for asking me, Simone.'

But any future visits would have to wait. The more she saw of Simone, the closer their relationship became, the more she risked distressing the girl with the news of her impending operation. Simone's behaviour cried out for a female role model and at this point in time

Ailee felt she was being dishonest by not disclosing what was going on in her life.

'I thought Dad might need adult reinforcements.' Simone narrowed her eyes, her glance going back and forth between the adults. 'I'll leave you two to say goodbye.'

'Thank you, Simone.' Fergus raised his eyebrows at Ailee and waited until his daughter was out of sight. 'When do we have this talk, Ailee Green?'

'Soon.'

'Early tomorrow morning?'

'I run in the mornings.'

'Ah, yes. I remember. Along Coogee beach.'

On Sunday morning, Ailee woke to a feeling of relief. The next time she saw Fergus she would explain about William and discuss why she needed to distance herself from Simone, at least until after the operation. Her heart pounded and suddenly the weight of the bedclothes on her chest was too heavy. She threw the covers off and sat up. She needed to get out of there because she couldn't sit still until it was done.

Dressed and with her hair tied back, the morning air cooled her face as she opened the front door and turned along the path towards the beach. She needed to be as healthy as possible before the operation to help her get over it more quickly. The scar from the nephrectomy would go a third of the way around her body and she would be doing little exercise for the next few weeks. She tried to consciously eat healthy foods and prepare herself to be in optimum fitness for the healing she'd need to do.

She'd been warned that the operation site pain would be considerable but there would be medication she could take for that, although if

Fergus performed the operation, the keyhole method was apparently less traumatic and shortened the recovery time.

Dr Harry was old-fashioned and the expert on open excisions. He believed there was less trauma to the donated kidney via the open method and Ailee was happy for William to have her kidney in the best condition it could be in.

The sun rose above the horizon and shone into her eyes.

It was earlier than she usually ran and not many other runners were up, which seemed unusual for the paths around Coogee.

Ahead, a lone figure sat on a bench overlooking the beach and there was something about the set of his shoulders that reminded her of Fergus.

Which, as she drew closer, made sense. Since it was him.

Ailee's heart began to pound as she came to a stop beside him. 'Fergus,' she said, and he turned to look at her.

'Ailee. Well met.' His glance warmed her already pink cheeks. He looked strong and fit but there were dark shadows beneath his eyes and her heart contracted.

Had she done this to him? He was a good man and didn't deserve being messed about. 'You're walking early. Why's that?' Although she thought she knew.

'Why am I out walking? I couldn't sleep. Why here? Someone I know lives around here and she told me she ran on this beach.'

'Come back for breakfast and then I'll drive you home,' she offered, not sure what she would tell her mother.

He smiled ruefully. 'Do I look that worn out?'

Ailee pretended to consider the question. 'Put it this way... I don't think you'll enjoy the long walk home.'

'How about we have a coffee here on the beach?' He pointed to the vendor setting up his stall.

'So much for my run,' Ailee complained, but she knew which she'd rather do and there were things she'd been waiting to say. Things she *had to* say. She paused for him to stand and as they crossed the street together, he rested his hand on the small of her back. As if he couldn't resist. His touch warmed her through her tee-Shirt and down to her toes.

When they were seated back on the bench with their takeaway coffees, neither seemed eager to start the conversation.

Ailee thought she had what she wanted to say ready. She'd practised her opening sentence enough to explain about William. It was the right thing to do. When he knew about her brother, she'd leave the decision to him.

'I'm sorry I kissed you on Friday,' he said.

Ailee's ready-for-departure train of thought derailed. That wasn't what she'd expected him to say. He was sorry? She looked right into his tired eyes. 'Why is that?'

He didn't say anything for a moment and, in fact, he really didn't have to say a word. The searing look he gave her made his words superfluous. 'Because I haven't slept well since Singapore and that made it worse. I want to do more than kiss you right now.'

He leant towards her and she found herself drawn closer as if pulled by an unseen force, but the moment was lost in a screech of tyres on the road behind them. Two horns blared at each other before the cars roared off in different directions.

Ailee and Fergus both winced and sighed with relief at the lack of impact, more aware than a lot of people about the fragility of life.

Ailee looked back at him. This was crazy. Fergus could melt her with one look and they were dancing around the attraction as if they had all the time in the world to choose to fall in love. People died. All the time. 'I'm not sorry you kissed me.'

'Oh, really?' His mouth lifted and the glint of humour made her lips twitch.

'Yep, but we have to talk. I do care for you but there are obstacles. I'm not backing away this time.'

His hand reached across the bench and lifted her fingers and turned them over palm-up. 'Fine. But let's do it somewhere more private. Simone went off last night to sleep at Peyton's house and won't be home until after lunch.'

He pulled her closer along the bench until her hip rested against his. 'Come home with me for a while.'

Her lips twitched. 'Are you propositioning me, Mr McVicker?'

He raised one eyebrow. 'My word, I am.' When he lifted her hand to his lips, she closed her eyes briefly just to feel it all.

He pressed his lips to her open palm, and the warm, tingling sensation travelled straight to her stomach where it still glowed from yesterday.

His voice dropped and seemed to brush against her skin. 'Why have we danced around this so long?'

'Because there are things you don't know and you won't listen.'

They stood. 'I promise to listen. But whatever I don't know can't change the feelings that I have for you.'

In unison they dropped their unfinished drinks into the waste bin and he squeezed her hand as they turned towards her house.

Her mother had dropped William at dialysis, and when Ailee ran in to collect her car keys there was no one to see her flushed cheeks. She dashed off a quick note to say she'd be home around lunchtime.

As they drove towards Clovelly, Ailee's cheeks warmed with the heat of his gaze fixed on her face. When she glanced across, he smiled and rested his long fingers on her leg as if to reassure himself she was there. It all felt so right. She looked down at his fingers curved around her thigh and grinned. 'Nobody has held my leg since high school.'

'I'd like to do a lot more but I'm playing it safe while you drive.'

'That seems a sensible idea. But no hanky panky until I tell you what's bothering me.'

'Then hanky panky?' His eyes were dancing and his hand slid.

She slapped him and laughed out loud just because she was with him. Suddenly the day shone brighter and more exciting than any she could remember.

He squeezed her leg briefly and then took his hand away. 'But until then it is incredibly difficult to behave myself.'

The tension mounted as they drove in through the gates and this time Fergus took her hand and led her around the back of the house and in through an enormous kitchen with a black slate floor.

Ailee followed, glad they didn't see anyone because Fergus took her straight up to his room with no pretence of conversation.

Her heart pounded and her mouth dried.

Fergus towed her into a bedroom similar in size to the one she'd been in on Friday, but this one was decorated in greens and blues and looked a little more lived-in. They stopped in the middle of the room and he captured her other hand so that she swung around and faced him.

He stared down into her eyes. 'I know we have to talk. But I also know it isn't going to change anything. I need you in my arms. So dreadfully. Can you wait?'

She shook her head in denial but her body leaned into him. 'No.'

Fergus smiled. His eyes intense, black and hungry. 'Should I ask you again?'

Her knees wobbled at his obvious intention and Ailee leaned up and brushed his mouth with hers before nodding. When his mouth came down Ailee sighed into him and one last thought wondered if she was so easily distracted, being a coward, because of the fear she wouldn't get this at all once the talking was done.

He lifted her and wrapped her in his arms. Homecoming. Like a burst of sunshine she'd been starved of. Like a hot blanket after the cold. Like love she'd waited for. And needed so desperately.

It seemed Fergus needed her, too.

His strength and gentleness created havoc as he slipped her tee from her shoulders, and slid the straps of her bra off her shoulders. Her bra hung precariously, holding her breasts loosely as he nibbled along her shoulders towards her neck and left her breasts bare to the coolness in the room.

She peeled the shirt from his shoulders with urgent fingers needing to feel his skin under her hands. With a final flurry of discarded clothes, he pulled her back onto the bed in his arms and rolled on top of her to stare down at her. His gaze swept over her like a blast of heat and she followed his glance down the length of their bodies.

This was what she wanted. So wanted. Needed. Had waited for and thought she'd lost. His legs lay on either side of hers as he held his weight off her body, his well-defined biceps golden and strong and so strongly beautiful he took her breath away.

Then he rolled and took her with him to lie on their sides facing each other, and this time when he kissed her there were no other thoughts except the taste and feel of Fergus's mouth on hers. The hunger between them exploded and expanded and left them both tossed and breathless.

When he finally lifted his mouth, she felt swollen and hot and just as hungry as he looked, but he moved down her body, nibbling down her neck before paying homage to her breasts, and she gasped and pulled him closer, harder against her. Time blurred and swirled as he worshipped with his hands and mouth until she ached for him.

He paused briefly to protect her before kneeling above her, and this time she lifted herself towards him. She opened her eyes as he entered her. She knew this man, this recent stranger, like she knew herself, and she gloried in his possession because he was her destiny. If not now, then some time that had to come for them in the future.

Afterwards they lay again on their sides, chests heaving, he still within her, staring at each other. He shook his head softly as he reached out and pulled the sheet over them.

Fergus was in shock. What had just happened? He felt like a survivor from a raging storm.

He'd loved his wife, had never been unfaithful, had never really expected to find love again. But this was no passing fancy. What Ailee had done to him had touched him deeply, resonated with a force unexpected, and he hoped she felt the same because he was hers for as long as they both shall live.

He tightened his hands on her shoulders and the thought of his recent possession made him stir again. Her eyes widened and she smiled cheekily at him.

Afterwards they fell asleep in each other's arms and when they woke it was lunchtime.

Fergus stirred first and he wondered, as he lay on his side and watched this woman wake for the second time in his life, what lay ahead of them. He hoped many more years of watching her wake up. It was a big call but he knew he was certain.

He grinned crookedly at her as she looked around the room properly for the first time. 'The room is a little sparse, I know, but for the first time with two people in it, the new bed is very comfortable,' Fergus said.

Nice. And thoughtful. She leaned over and kissed him for the kindness. A new bed. She wondered when he'd bought it.

She rolled onto her back and avoided his eyes. They'd entered each other's souls back there and their intimacy made her blush so deeply her hands came up to cover the heat in her cheeks.

'How on earth did we come to this point with each other so quickly? I can't believe I'm here with you.' She glanced down at the sheet covering her body. 'Like this.'

'Neither can I,' he said huskily as he moved closer until his shoulder touched hers again. 'Stuff that dreams are made of.' He smiled at her. 'I haven't been alive like this for a very long time.' His gaze swept over her and tingled her skin with his look of adoration.

Ailee wanted to believe him. His words fitted the moment perfectly and Fergus was everything she'd dreamed of in a lover and in a man. Gentle, yet powerful, and the way he worshipped her body made her feel as if she was the most beautiful woman in the world.

He kissed her and this time the fire was quick to sweep over them. 'I have so needed you against me,' he murmured as his lips burnt a trail down her neck and Ailee arched into him as his mouth closed over the peak of her breast.

She dug her fingers into the strength of his shoulder blades and then down his back, remembering...

'You are so beautiful,' he sighed into the hollow between her breasts, and Ailee held his head and pulled him back towards her, and they lay on their sides again, staring at each other, and Fergus pulled the sheet up and over their heads so that they lay in their own world, holding hands in the white-out.

The sun shone through the tree outside the window and dappled their tent as it billowed.

'Okay,' he said softly. 'What do you need to tell me?'

Ailee looked at the man beside her, the strong planes of his face carved in relief by shadows, his beautiful mouth that could give so much heat, and his caring eyes that made tears spring to her own. Of course Fergus would understand and support her.

'It's about my brother. William.'

Fergus nodded.

Before she could say another word, the insistent tone of his pager sounded and the moment was shattered by the outside world.

Fergus closed his eyes for a second and then his lips curved ruefully. 'I'm not on call. Stay here. I'll be back.'

He slid from beneath the sheet and then covered Ailee's shoulder as he sat on the edge of the bed. He picked up the phone and with his other hand he tucked the sheet around her neck.

Ailee watched him, watched his face, listened to his voice and decoded the expressions on his face. He'd have to go and they would postpone this again, but her time would come and everything would be fine. Her doubts had gone.

Fergus replaced the receiver. 'There's a problem. I do have to go.'

'I know.'

He leant across and kissed her forehead. 'Do you want to stay here?'

'No. I'll go home.'

'I'll phone you. I broke my word. There is no doubt we have to talk.' Fergus glanced around at the clothes scattered across the floor and his eyes twinkled. 'We do seem to have trouble keeping our clothes on around each other.'

She blushed but held her head high to meet his teasing. 'It's a lovely failing.'

Ailee slid out of the bed and wrapped the sheet around her body as he moved into the dressing room. She stood up, gathered her clothes and began to dress.

William was home when she came in and he brushed Ailee's concern off and went to bed, complaining of cramps. Fergus rang to ask her out for dinner, but Ailee couldn't help the feeling that something was wrong with William and she needed to get to the bottom of it. She couldn't leave William while he was unwell.

She could hear the dissatisfaction with her evasion in his voice through the phone. 'Your brother is sick?' Ailee knew she sounded distracted, which wasn't like her. 'Is there anything I can do?'

'Not yet, but maybe later.' She heard the dryness in her tone.

'I'll see you at work Monday, then,' he said.

'Thank you for understanding, Fergus.'

By tea time William was still unwell, which was unusual after resting. Ailee nagged her reluctant brother into a return to the hospital for a check-up.

Her years of renal medicine blurred when William was involved, but she suspected her brother's condition could cause more delays for their surgery. He needed to be well by Wednesday's assessment clinic or who knew what Fergus would decide?

William was admitted to hospital as an emergency and the duty doctor refused to meet Ailee's eyes and asked her to leave while he carried out the examination.

Ailee paced. But when the doctor had finished, William also avoided her eyes, seeming even more subdued, and Ailee wanted to ask for her brother's medical records so she could find out why. But she didn't. She'd promised William years ago she wouldn't without his permission. Something told her that permission wouldn't be forthcoming this time.

When the duty doctor came to see her, further evasion ensued. 'We'll keep William in. I think it's best if you see Mr McVicker in the morning and discuss your brother with him tomorrow. Go home, Dr Green. Will asked you not to come back.'

Ailee's sinking feeling that not all was right with William strengthened.

First thing on Monday morning, Ailee heard Jody had been readmitted through Casualty with signs of rejection of her new kidney and pancreas, which meant Ailee had no chance to talk to Fergus.

Every staff member on the ward was on tenterhooks as they waited for their star patient to arrive, and Ailee went about her duties with a dark heart.

First William unwell and now Jody. Ailee met Fergus's eyes as Jody was wheeled into the ward and they both knew she was headed for High Dependency.

Jody lay in the emergency bed and she looked terrible. Her face brightly flushed and the rigors of her body were shaking the rails on the bed in time to the chattering of her teeth. 'Get some bloods and get another line in,' Fergus said as he reached for the phone. 'Who sent her to the ward? She needs to get to ICU immediately.'

Jody opened her eyes and squinted up a Fergus. 'Don't let me reject my kidney, Mr McVicker. I so want to be well. I don't want to let my donor down.'

'You haven't let anyone down, Jody. We'll do everything we can. Try and rest, sweetheart. Close your eyes and leave it to us.'

The ward round was postponed and, like the emergency with Emma, Ailee itched to be back on the medical team and follow Fergus and Jody up to Intensive Care.

But she had her own important work to do. The next few hours would be critical. Jody could lose at least her kidney, if not the pancreas, and if infection set in they would have to fight hard not to lose Jody.

In her office, Ailee tried to concentrate on the paperwork essential to the donor-recipient records and even managed to complete the full list of recipients for Marion and John's daughter, Eva, which she would need later in the day.

Ailee was scheduled to meet Eva's parents after lunch. Already she had three thank-you letters to give to them from the families of people whose lives had been enormously changed by Eva's gift.

All through the morning Ailee buried herself in the tasks she needed to complete and when she finally made her way to Intensive Care, Jody was on life support and her family was there.

Fergus had just left to do a delayed ward round and that meant Ailee couldn't stay. She hugged Jody's mother and hurried back to the ward.

By the time she arrived, Fergus had started the round without her. She came in as Fergus and Lawrence were discussing his discharge.

'If you feel your spirits dropping, you need to contact your support worker,' Fergus said.

Lawrence looked up and smiled at Ailee. 'Hi, Ailee. Have you told Mr McVicker what you've got me doing now?'

Fergus glanced across and gave Ailee a half-smile as if he wasn't willing to broadcast to the world how glad he was to see her. Apparently her being late wasn't a problem now. The thought made her smile.

'I haven't had a chance this morning.' She looked at Fergus. 'Lawrence has enrolled in a correspondence welfare course, and is offering to mentor some of the young patients we have with compliance problems as soon as he finishes his course. If they listen to anyone, it will be someone who understands like Lawrence does.'

'Sounds promising. Keep me posted. Well done, both of you.' The entourage moved on and William was next.

'Not been well, William?'

William shook his head and closed lacklustre eyes.

'Let's have a look at you, then.' Rita stepped in and pulled the curtains around Fergus, William and herself.

Ailee sighed and stared at the screens around her brother and she could hear Fergus murmuring. When the curtains opened she looked up to see the verdict.

'If we can get him a little better, I think we'll be fine for next week. But a lot of that will be up to you, William.'

Ailee sighed with relief and then Fergus went on, 'Contact his donor.' He scanned down the page for the donor's name, it was right at the back, and his fingers stilled. His face froze. He closed his eyes. When he opened them there was an arctic wind blowing straight at her.

'Any relation?' The question ignored everyone else in the room and it seemed time slowed to a frame at a time as Fergus's eyes bored into hers.

Ailee felt as though she was on the witness stand but she'd done nothing wrong. She lifted her chin. 'Me. I'm the donor.'

'And William?' Fergus's eyes burned into hers.

Ailee looked at William sitting up in bed, pale and listless and watching both of them. 'Is my only brother.'

Chapter 17

Fergus

Fergus felt as though all the air had been sucked out of the room and a tight band across his chest wouldn't allow him to breathe in again. The hospital walls seemed whiter, the faces around him faded as he gazed into Ailee's green eyes. Fear gripped him and his mouth grew tight to hold it in.

He looked away from the woman he'd only recently admitted to himself he loved, and breathed, dragged his gaze to focus on her brother.

He tried to think. It all made sense. 'I see.'

But how had he not seen?

William had Ailee's colouring but had missed out on her height. He had a similar smile to his sister, though, and now that he really looked he could see a likeness in the set of their chins.

This made it even harder for Fergus to grapple with what he'd just learned, but now wasn't the time for him. The whole team watched and to frogmarch Ailee into his office would not be a good look. The rest of the group did not give the impression this was startling news so he gathered he'd been the only one in the dark.

Fergus turned to Rita, who was trying valiantly to appear uninterested in the byplay between Ailee and himself. 'Make sure Dr Green has the final blood tests and cross-match attended.'

Rita nodded in response.

He turned back to William and met his eyes. 'I'll be keeping an eye on your results, too, young man. You'd better stay in hospital tonight as well.'

'If I have to.' The words were quiet but almost sullen as if he wanted to leave the place for ever.

William wasn't happy... well, he wasn't the only one. Fergus hoped he could see that it wasn't up for negotiation.

Ailee stood biting her lip and he resisted the ridiculous impulse to put his hand up to stop her.

Regret shone from her eyes as she searched his face, but he knew it wasn't her fault he'd found out this way. He hadn't given her a chance to tell him. He'd been too focused on getting her into his arms, into his bed, into his life.

But still shock rattled through him. He'd have to worry about that later because he was moving on to the next room and he needed this round done so he could think.

The next couple beamed at him. Peter and Emma were both doing well and served to redirect the focus.

'How are you, Emma?' Fergus forced his lips up in acknowledgement of the young woman's improvement. Emma already had more colour in her cheeks.

'So much better. This would have been my dialysis day and I didn't have to go.'

'New kidneys are clever organs.' This time the smile came easier and Fergus glanced through her chart. Good scenarios did happen.

'Everything is perfect. Just get your strength back. You should be able to go home next week if all goes well.'

'What about you, Peter?' In fact, the young man looked pale. Fergus concentrated on the donor more than he might have ten minutes ago. Dark insight into his own shortcomings?

Fergus realised he'd always been concerned that the donor recovered well but his obsession had been the recipient. From the donor's point of view, they'd done the job. With the news of Ailee's plan to be a donor that thought process had already begun a shift in focus.

'I'm fine, Mr McVicker. When can I go home?'

Fergus narrowed his eyes. The young man seemed to be quite exhausted and was in obvious discomfort. 'Is there a rush?'

Peter smiled weakly. 'Not really. It's just my dad is finding it hard to run the shop and if I even went in and sat there, I could help a little.'

'You can't do a lot for a few weeks at the very least, Peter. You've had a major operation and at a guess,' Fergus narrowed his gaze, 'you're not taking enough pain medication.' Fergus glanced at Rita, who confirmed his suspicion with a nod.

Peter said, 'It makes me sleepy.'

'That's right. Take it. Sleep. Recover. That's an order.'

Peter looked sheepishly at Fergus and smiled slightly. 'If you say so.'

Fergus turned to Rita. 'Please ensure Peter takes his analgesics on a regular basis. The weight of the world will wait till he's a little better.' He looked at the distance between the two beds. 'And can we push those beds together the next time they get up so they can hold hands?'

Everybody smiled at Fergus's directive.

Peter asked, 'How long do you reckon we'll be holding hands here?'

'Home at the end of this week if all goes well.'

Fergus didn't feel like bonhomie but it wasn't anyone else's fault except his. But and as soon as the round was over he intended to have a little chat with Dr Ailee Green.

A few minutes later the group broke up and Fergus took Ailee's arm and steered her into the office. He ignored the furtive looks from the others and shut the door to the ward.

The air in the room seemed to shimmer in front of his eyes as he tried to remain calm and collected.

'Let's go back to when we spent time together in Singapore.' He waited for a moment, as if she needed time to recall, before he went on. 'Why didn't you tell me you were booked as a live donor and that was the reason you didn't want to see me in Sydney?'

Ailee brushed hair from her eyes. He'd wanted to do that himself but didn't trust himself to touch her.

A pulse beat in her throat and he puffed out a breath. It wasn't her fault. She'd tried to tell him yesterday and he'd distracted her from the conversation.

He turned away. Hiding his own conflicted emotions. Anger, frustration, culpability, protectiveness, fear.

She stepped around him so she could see his face. Lifted her chin in that fearless way she had that made him want to bury his face in her hair and pull her to him. To draw strength and courage that she had in spades.

Her eyes met his. 'If I'd known you were a leading renal specialist in Sydney, then Singapore would have been a very different experience.' She tilted her chin. 'You avoided the information. As I did! In Singapore my impending operation wasn't something I discussed with passing strangers.'

Fergus shook his head. 'We were more than strangers!'

Ailee raised her chin higher. 'Passing holiday romance, you mean?'

He looked away and he knew that what she'd said was true.

Her hand reached out and gently she poked him in the chest. 'I had to be here to support my mother and William, to be the strong one and not divert their attention from any effects on me for the next few months. I chose to deal with one issue at a time and if that put paid to a liaison with a man I met on the plane, then so be it.'

'This is why you're doing a temporary job,' he said as this realisation struck. 'Because you'll be off work for the next couple of months, recovering?'

'Every job in this unit matters. They had no one for coordinator at short notice. I was still technically on leave, and if I filled that position I could see the unit from another important angle. It's the least I can do for the unit that has saved my brother and taught me so much.'

'And the last week you couldn't tell me?'

'I've been trying for the last three days.'

'Earlier would have been better.' But he knew that wasn't fair. Said more mildly, 'When I met William as a patient the first time would have been the perfect time.'

'Yes, but sadly I was still reeling from your appointment.'

He laughed without humour. 'Define irony. A kidney surgeon falls for a live donor and she's reluctant to risk a relationship because she's donating a kidney.'

'The main concern was that you and your daughter don't need another tragedy in your lives.'

His face twisted into a cynical smile. 'Simone is definitely a concern. I understand we need to respect the boundary between work and personal matters and I apologise for not doing that in the past.' He thought of that office kiss, way out of line! 'But we do need to talk, Ailee. When we finish at five?'

She inclined her head.

'Perhaps leave your car here and drive somewhere? Then I'll drop you back?'

'Fine.' His Ailee looked pale but composed and his heart ached.

'Thank you.' Now for the harder part. 'I want a repeat psychological and psychiatric assessment done on William A.S.A.P.'

She frowned. 'This could slow everything down again. He's already had one, a few months ago.'

Perhaps she wasn't seeing what he was. 'And he can have another. I have concerns he may not be mentally ready for this.'

Two spots of colour appeared on her cheeks. 'I can't believe what I'm hearing. You can't postpone our operations!'

'I'll pretend you didn't say that, Doctor,' Fergus said very quietly.

He walked out of the room, and then the ward, around the side of the hospital and down to the shady area reserved for smokers. Thankfully, the area was deserted, and he could have a few moments to himself.

Lord knew, he needed time to come to grips with this.

Live donor. People did it all the time. He advocated it. He'd travelled halfway across the world in a flimsy metal cylinder to discover new ways to promote live donations in Australia.

Now he had one on his own doorstep that he actively wanted to halt. Ailee's gift to her brother was everything he encouraged and it was ripping his heart out, tearing against everything he believed in.

"Tragic irony" weren't big enough words. Would it have been better if he'd known this yesterday before he'd taken Ailee home to his bed? Would he have distanced himself from her because of this?

No. That was inevitable. Undeniable.

It was the shock and he could even begin to see her side of the dilemma with his profession. His life's work. He knew the risks, understood now why she left his hotel room, why'd she'd tried to deny their fierce attraction. But she might as well have tried to flap her arms back to Sydney because he doubted anything could have prevented their desire from igniting.

He'd been totally smitten by Ailee since Singapore and this enormous bump in their road to happiness didn't change the way he felt about her.

But this sure as hell complicated things.

Especially with Simone.

Concern about Ailee's operation was the last thing his daughter needed now she'd started to trust him again.

Simone was going to be a mess.

And he'd be a mess right alongside her.

Until all of this was over.

Chapter 18

Ailee

Ailee sagged back against the wall of the office as Fergus left the room. And it felt as if he took all of the air with him.

Everything she'd tried to prevent since Singapore had happened anyway. Fergus had been hurt by her lack of disclosure, they'd still fallen deeply for each other and now he was frightened for her. Would be frightened for Simone as soon as he had time to think about it. She'd seen it in his eyes. Had wanted to comfort him.

Until he'd said William needed a new psychological assessment. And yes, she'd been silly to rear up at that. Talk about an emotional morning. Fergus was the lead surgeon and had full rights to ask for any test he wanted.

But that didn't change the fact Fergus had found out in the worst possible way and now he was angry with her. But despite everything, she knew he wouldn't take it out on William. That thought was just as unfair as this whole situation was to both of them. She'd seen what a fine human being he was. How much he cared for his patients. She shook her head. No.

He wouldn't.

Ailee walked out of the office and straight into Rita.

Rita took one look at her and glanced around to see if anyone else had noticed Ailee's pallor. 'You okay, kiddo?'

'I'm fine.' Such a trite word and so untrue.

'So he wasn't thrilled to find you were the donor?'

How much did Rita guess? 'I think he's just disappointed I didn't tell him beforehand, seeing as I work here and everyone else knew.'

'Disappointment?' Rita snorted. 'Is that what it was?'

'He does have a point, given our working relationship.' And our private one.

Rita didn't look convinced by her lame attempt at an explanation but she didn't labour the point. 'What time is your appointment with the Ellises?'

Ailee looked at her watch. 'Another half-hour, but before then I need to check on one last recipient. Oh, and Rita, we need to arrange another psychological and psychiatric assessment of William on Mr McVicker's orders.'

'I'll do that.'

Rita didn't seem to think it unusual that Fergus had requested a repeat assessment. Maybe she was being paranoid.

She heard herself say "Mr McVicker" when she thought of him as Fergus and that sounded strange, too. It wasn't the only thing weird about her relationship with Fergus but one of many.

She didn't have time or the headspace to worry about it. Separating workspace and personal issues was important, if difficult, given how the boundaries had been crossed with William/her operations even without the developing relationship (if that's what it was) with Fergus. She'd find out where she stood soon enough. Five o'clock, to be exact.

'If you hear any more about Jody, let me know, will you?' Ailee glanced at her watch again. It was time she headed back to her office.

Her problems were nothing compared to those of the couple she was about to see.

The Ellises looked worn down by grief, and Ailee hugged them both before directing them to the two chairs in front of her desk. 'Thank you so much for coming.'

With a heavy sigh, Marion sat. 'I know you said you'd come to us, Ailee, but we needed to get out. This visit gave us some purpose today.'

Mr Ellis rubbed his hand over his lips back and forward. Back and forward, as he sat beside his wife. Ailee could see the skin had peeled with his actions. 'We're finding it hard to start the day at the moment. Everyone tells us that in time we'll remember more good times, but we're not there yet.'

Ailee felt helpless in the face of their grief. There was so little she could do to ease their pain. 'Nobody expects you to be able to function normally.'

Marion said, 'We don't even have an idea what normal is anymore.'

'No. I'm so sorry.' Ailee shuffled the papers in her hand. 'Would you like to know about the recipients? I do have three letters here from the families of recipients whose lives have been changed. Please, don't read them until you feel you're able to.'

Marion looked at her husband and then back at Ailee and nodded. 'Tell us a little if you can, please, Ailee. We'll read them later.'

'I can tell you that Eva has saved the life of a fifteen- year-old-girl with cystic fibrosis. This young woman would have died within the next week or two if not for Eva. Her parents are beside themselves with joy that she will now get better.'

Marion smiled with great effort. 'That is wonderful news. Isn't it, John?'

John nodded, unable to speak, and reached into his pocket for his handkerchief.

Marion sniffed and lifted her chin a little higher. 'Is there more you can tell us?'

'One of Eva's kidneys and her pancreas went to a twenty-two-year-old woman in Melbourne who is studying to be a doctor and had been sick for two years. She was also a diabetic, like the girl I told you about last week, so had the double transplant. She is doing so well she may go home at the end of next week. Hopefully Eva's gift will mean she will save more lives well into the future.'

They were all silent for a moment as they tried to envisage what it meant to the recipient.

Ailee went on because she decided it would be better to get it all over as soon as possible. 'The other kidney went to a twenty-five-year-old man whose wife had died. He has two little boys, so the difference to that family is incredible.'

Marion looked at her husband. 'Imagine if we hadn't agreed and all that good was wasted.'

Mr Ellis nodded. His eyes red.

'It's such a hard and incredibly brave decision,' Ailee said.

'Are they the only ones?' John had recovered his composure and was trying hard to support his wife.

'There is one more. The other person is a thirty-year- old woman, struck down with keratoconus, which is an eye disease where the central cornea bulges forward and prevents light from being focused correctly into the eye.'

Ailee sketched a quick diagram of an eye to explain the problem. 'The only substitute for replacing a human cornea is a human cornea.' She looked up to see that they understood.

'This lady has been blind for eighteen months, lost her job and struggled to look after herself, and now, thanks to Eva, has had her sight restored and can lead a normal life.'

Ailee handed across an envelope. 'All the information I can give you is on that sheet but I think it would be too much to take in now. Just know that you did the right thing and Eva has irrevocably touched these people's lives and she will never, ever, be forgotten.'

'And we can't contact them, can we?'

'No. I'm sorry.' Ailee shook her head. 'But I can send on any letters they or you want to send and there is an independent register you can leave your name with. Later, if any of the recipients want to contact you, they can register with them as well.'

'We'll think about it.' John nodded and looked at Marion. 'A few months down the track perhaps.'

'Don't rush anything.' Ailee smiled gently. 'You can ring me any time. If I'm not available, someone else will get back to you as soon as they can. I understand Eva's funeral is tomorrow?'

'That's why we came back so fast.' John cleared his throat. 'We wanted to tell people about the families Eva's request has helped. Maybe then even more people will agree to sign donor cards in the future.'

Marion added. 'That way Eva's legacy will continue to grow.' Marion leant forward to lever herself up from her chair and her husband jumped up to help her.

Ailee stood as well. 'That is a wonderful idea. I will be thinking of you all tomorrow.'

'Thank you for your help, Ailee.'

Ailee touched their shoulders. 'Thank you from everyone here. Me, Mr McVicker, all the staff and especially the people whose lives Eva has changed.'

Ailee watched them go and sighed. She remembered when her father had died suddenly and her family had gone through the shocking grief that surrounded the loss of a loved one.

The gathering of family, friends and even strangers had helped more than she'd believed possible. She hoped it would be that way for the Ellises tomorrow.

Her phone rang and it was a transplant co-ordinator from a southern Sydney hospital with a kidney available for one of her patients on the waiting list. Another tragedy much like the Ellises'. Ailee couldn't help wincing, but it was another ray of hope for those in need.

Ailee looked up her records and dialled the number of the proposed recipient.

Thirty-eight-year-old Dan Chang had been on dialysis for three years while he'd waited for a kidney and he couldn't believe it when Ailee phoned him with the news.

'So I have to come in now?' Dan's voice betrayed his disbelief and growing excitement.

'Yes, please, Dan. As soon as you can without getting a speeding ticket. You're only about half an hour away. Don't eat or drink anything and we'll start workup as soon as you get here.'

'I'm on my way. Wait till I tell my wife.'

Ailee smiled at the waves of exhilaration coming through the phone. 'Just remember, sometimes things change. Don't get over-excited until we can guarantee you're going in.'

'I'll try not to, but it's hard. See you soon.'

Ailee phoned Rita to prepare the ward first. Coward.

Rita was quick to answer and too soon there was Fergus to be notified. And the in-charge nurse in theatre. Fergus would ring the anaesthetists.

When her phone rang she knew it was Fergus answering his page, her throat closed, she couldn't speak for a second as she gathered her thoughts.

'Did you page me, Ailee?'

Ailee licked dry lips. 'Yes. We have a donor kidney and match available for today. What time would you like theatre organised for?'

'Make it two this afternoon. That should give the recipient time to fast and have the work-up. I'll have my secretary reschedule the afternoon appointments in my rooms for later.'

Ailee hesitated and wondered if she, too, would get a reprieve.

Fergus must have read her mind. His voice dropped. 'We do need to talk. But yes, I'll be later than intended. May I pick you up from your place at eight? If I'm late, I'll still be coming.'

Ailee swallowed. 'We could put that off until tomorrow if that makes it easier for you.'

'No,' he said succinctly. 'Anything else?'

Ailee pulled a face at the phone but her voice remained composed. 'That's all, thank you.'

'I'll see you tonight, then.'

The call ended and Ailee put her own phone down. Today was going to be another big day.

Ailee gathered the enormous amounts of paperwork needed for Dan Chang's transplant operation and headed for the ward. She couldn't help going over the conversation she'd just had with Fergus as she walked, and she reasoned that if he'd considered her planned operation an insurmountable problem he wouldn't be in that much of a hurry to clear the air.

Maybe everything wasn't as bad as she thought it was.

Fergus arrived at Ailee's house at exactly eight p.m. Ailee knew because she'd been watching the clock for the last hour and she'd only just checked the time again.

'I'm going out now, Mum,' she called through to the sitting room where Helen sat watching television.

The doorbell rang before she could get to it and she muttered under her breath. She'd hoped to keep Fergus and her mother apart. Ailee opened the door before Fergus had finished ringing. 'I'm ready. Let's go.'

'What's your rush?' He looked tall and gorgeous and totally in command and refused to move away from the door. 'I'd like to meet your mother.'

Ailee glared at him, but she was really annoyed at herself for being so glad to see him standing there when she should be ushering him away at warp speed.

'Who's there, dear?' Helen's voice floated through to the front door.

Fergus just stared back with slightly raised eyebrows. 'Don't you think there have been enough secrets, Ailee?' he said.

Ailee sighed and turned to call over her shoulder. 'It's Fergus McVicker.' She resisted the urge to grit her teeth at Fergus. 'Would you like to meet him?'

Helen appeared and Ailee moved back to allow Fergus to step into the tiled entry.

Fergus smiled warmly and held out his hand. 'Hello, Mrs Green. I'm Fergus. I work with Ailee.' He shook hands and Ailee's mother blushed prettily.

'Call me Helen. It's lovely to finally meet you, Fergus. You've featured in a lot of our conversations this week.'

Fergus lifted his eyebrows and looked at Ailee. 'Really?'

Helen nodded. 'William is a constant concern at the moment, as you know.'

'I understand that. He's lucky to have such a supportive family.' The words were sincere with no hidden meanings that she could hear.

Had he come to peace with her decision already? Maybe she had worried too much.

Ailee glanced at her watch. 'I won't be long, Mum.'

Her mother leaned in and kissed her. 'Take your time, honey. I'm off to bed now anyway.' She smiled up at their visitor. 'Nice to meet you, Fergus.'

He held out his hand and shook hers. 'Good to meet you, too, Helen.'

Ailee watched her mother colour again and she sympathised. Fergus at his charming best was quite something to behold, but Ailee was learning to hide the effect.

Finally seated in the car, the silence pulled like a piece of toffee – stretching out until something felt like it would break. Ailee drew a breath to make her feelings known but he spoke first.

'I have to call in at the hospital. Our new recipient is good, but I want to check Jody one more time tonight.'

The other young recipient had been at the back of Ailee's mind all evening so she readily agreed. 'Can I come up to the ward with you? Just to have a peek. I won't go in and see her.'

He nodded with his eyes on the road. 'I don't have a problem with that.'

When they arrived at the hospital Ailee followed Fergus up to Intensive Care, where he gowned and gloved before entering the isolation room. Jody was being treated with huge doses of steroids and the strongest immunosuppressants to prevent her body rejecting the donor kidney, but it left Jody's system easy prey to bacteria and viruses.

Ailee spoke to the registered nurse at the desk, one she'd known a long time, and watched Fergus through the glass as he spoke to Jody and the nurse specialling her.

Ailee inclined her head at the window. 'So, she's improving?'

The nurse touched her arm. 'She's looking better, Ailee. When he was here earlier, Mr McVicker seemed to think this acute rejection phase was settling. Her observations are stable and her counts are down.'

Ailee could see that Fergus was preparing to leave. 'Fingers crossed. I'll pop up and see her parents tomorrow.'

The nurse nodded. 'So, what are you doing here after hours? Are you with Mr McVicker for fun, or are there more transplants on the cards?'

They both looked across at the other glassed-in room.

Ailee forced a smile. Frivolity was far from her mind. 'Not for fun, but no more transplants tonight so far. How is our latest patient? Is Dan stable?'

'Looking good. His wife's a sweetie. They're a lovely couple. New transplants are thrilling to watch for, and we're all doing what we can to see the good result continues.'

'I know you do. You're all fabulous.' Ailee nodded, aware that Fergus stood waiting for her. 'Better go. Thanks for your help.'

Ailee crossed the room and hoped the nurse assumed they were there together on renal business because she wasn't ready to be the subject of a gossip storm. She'd worked long enough in medicine to know how quickly relationship rumours spread.

'Shall I take your arm?' Fergus teased, well aware Ailee was trying to give the impression everything was businesslike between them.

'No, thank you. I have to work here. You'll be going back to your own hospital in a week or two.'

'A good thing,' Fergus said quietly.

Ailee looked across at him and tried to push down the unexpected hurt that statement caused.

They didn't speak again until Fergus pulled up outside a trendy restaurant overlooking the moonlit beach at Coogie. 'I thought a late supper would be in order as I haven't eaten. You could have dessert if you're not hungry.'

Ailee bit her lip. He'd been working non-stop. She hadn't thought of that. 'That would be lovely. Of course you have to eat. Now I feel guilty I didn't offer you something when you came to pick me up.'

'Guilt is good.' He smiled and the wicked teasing in his eyes made her heart pitter patter too darned hard. The man was irresistible to her. Fergus held the door of the restaurant open for her.

Did this mean he wasn't upset with her anymore?

Banter was good.

Flash restaurants were nice too. She could get used to waiters rushing to assist her. They were seated quickly at a reserved table and Ailee glanced around at the few couples still seated.

'This is very stylish,' Ailee said. 'I was thinking you'd want somewhere more private to vent your feelings.'

'I'm a very stylish guy,' he mocked, 'and if I took you back to my home, I wasn't sure we'd get any talking done.'

Ailee willed the heat not to rise in her face but her cheeks burned. 'It takes two.'

'Absolutely,' Fergus said, straight-faced, and caught the waiter's eye to order. 'Much more fun.'

Ailee chose a sorbet and Fergus a rare steak and salad and the food arrived in minutes. They discussed Jody's stabilisation and Dan's operation, and the rapport between them felt so robust and satisfying, and reminded her how good it was to have Fergus to bounce ideas off.

As soon as he'd finished eating, Fergus didn't skirt the issue. They needed to tackle this head-on.

'So what are we going to do about this deadly attraction between us?'

Ailee looked down at the remains of her melted into a mango puddle in the bottom of the glass dish sorbet. 'Is the attraction deadly?'

Fergus waited patiently, not answering, until she was forced to look at him to break the silence. Only then did he say, 'I admit to some brief homicidal thoughts when I discovered the tiny fact you hadn't mentioned.'

Ailee lifted her chin. 'You said any secret I had wouldn't change the way you felt.'

'And I meant it.' He allowed his words to settle between them and sink in. Ailee felt the weight slide off her shoulders like a scarf onto the floor.

He changed tack. 'Why was it so hard for you to tell me about William?'

She turned her head and stared out the window, beyond the dark night sand to the moonlight sparkling off the waves. Then back at him. Meeting his eyes. 'I don't entirely know, but meeting you threw my world into turmoil. I wasn't thinking straight, I can see that now. You have that effect on me.' She half laughed but without much amusement. Pulled her coffee cup closer.

'And later?'

'Then when you turned up at the hospital and I had no warning, I didn't think at all.'

His eyes bored into hers. 'Why didn't you think I'd be there for you?' She had his full attention.

Her shoulders creaked when she moved them in the tiny shrug. Her neck tight. She tried to remember all the reasons but it was so hard with him, so big, and gorgeous and looking at her with heat in his eyes despite this conversation. 'The next few weeks of discomfort I'll be unattractive company. I'll have physical restrictions for the first few months and I guess I'll have changes in body image to come to terms with, although they're minor considerations.'

'Not too minor when it's your own body.' His hand came over and brushed hers. Fleeting but as if he couldn't help himself yet didn't want to distract her from her thoughts. 'Though, know that I will see you as completely beautiful through it all.'

Ailee's breath caught with his gentle touch and his words. She glanced back at him, but he waved her on.

She took another breath and pushed forward. Glad to. 'I won't have time for distractions. William has to be watched closely and I'll need to stay on standby until he's right. I don't want what happened to Emma to happen to William.'

His brows lifted. 'Not everyone has a sister who specialises in renal surgery and those recipients seem to survive. You haven't convinced me.'

Perhaps. 'Well, that full commitment to my family is no way to start a relationship with someone.'

He smiled. It was a little tight around the corners, but his eyes had softened more. 'But we're not starting are we. We've begun. I'm sure we'll cope.'

Did that mean they were still on? She inhaled and of course his aftershave came with the scent of coffee and warm male. Her belly loosened a little. She did so want to be with this man. 'All right, then. I didn't presume that. Mostly I don't think it's fair to you and Simone. There are risks, not huge risks statistically, but risks nevertheless.'

She was glad to get this off her chest. 'You've already told me how long it's taken Simone to resume normal life after losing her mother. If she were to see me debilitated, it is likely I could bring all those painful memories back for her. I don't want to cause her,' she raised her eyes to him, 'or you, pain.'

There. She'd said it. She blew out a breath and played with her coffee spoon.

Fergus took a few moments to reply and then he spoke slowly, as if being careful of what he said. 'I can see that Simone's distress is a distinct possibility and something I need to address. It was one of the first things I thought about when I finally found out William was your brother.'

He held her gaze. Not shirking the biggest point for him. 'Simone is to be protected at all costs.'

Ailee agreed.

These were all reasons she should have stayed away from him in Singapore. Funny how the closer she became to Fergus the more obstacles she could see. And the more she desired him. All of him. The man.

'Why didn't you want me to meet your mother this evening?' His question jolted her out of her meanderings, and she spoke without thought.

'Simone isn't the only one who needs protecting. My mother dreams of me settled with children and you're any potential mother-in-law's dream son-in-law.'

'Touché.'

She saw Fergus acknowledge the hit and Ailee sighed and went on. 'Why broadcast my somewhat tenuous relationship with you before William's operation? If Mum thought I was entering an affair, she would revisit the possible ramifications on my life, fertility, and health again. And again.'

'I'm guessing she's said so many times?' When Ailee nodded Fergus pursed his lips. Such wonderful lips. 'Your mother is entitled to her valid concerns.'

Ailee waved her hand. 'You're the last person I'd expect to be unenthusiastic about live donors.' She speared him with a glance. 'Do you have concerns?'

'Honestly?' He looked across at her and she saw the way his eyes softened. He did care. She suspected he cared a lot and the thought warmed her deep inside. But his answer here was important. 'If I didn't know you so well, the statistics tell me there's very little to worry about, or about one in thirty thousand as in any operation. Knowing you doesn't change that, but somehow it does.'

He glanced out the window and then back at Ailee. 'I'd be lying if I said I wasn't worried. I've already lost someone dear to me from a much lower risk operation.' He drew an audible breath before continuing. 'But I can see you're determined and I'll be glad, as you will be, when it's all over.'

He seemed to hesitate, as if unsure about voicing what was on his mind. 'If the operation goes ahead, that is.'

Ailee felt so unutterably relieved to finally have her concerns out in the open that there was a delay before she comprehended his last sentence. He was watching her. She could feel it. AS if waiting. And then the words sank in.

Her gaze flew to his. 'What do you mean, *if* the operation goes ahead? We're booked in next week.'

Fergus spread his fingers on the table. 'You haven't seen the paperwork. William's psychological assessment wasn't good. I don't know how everyone missed it, but William is exhibiting all the signs of denial and non-compliance.'

Ailee shook her head vehemently. 'No, he's not!'

Fergus's voice softened but she heard the note of authority. 'You know we have to be sure he's not going to throw this chance away. To be reassured he won't break the very stringent rules and medication regime post-operatively. We do him no favours if we allow him to waste this chance.'

'I can't believe what I'm hearing.' She shook her head, hair swishing and irritating her face, cold in her throat where only moments ago there had been heat. Disbelief in her voice. 'How dare you say William is non-compliant? He's never missed a clinic or dialysis and Lord knows, it's painful enough for him.'

Implacable Fergus stared back. 'I'm responsible for the optimum outcome for my patients. Like hell I'll waste your kidney if your brother isn't going to value it as he should.'

Ailee thought her head would explode. 'What?' She hissed the word and heads turned.

His voice remained calm and quiet as if they were discussing nothing emotive. 'William has been binge-drinking alcohol. Eating the wrong foods. His results confirm it. His fluid quota has been consistently over and his biochemistry is totally out of whack.'

Ailee felt as if someone had punched her chest. Her heart ached with horror. No. This wasn't right. She shook her head slowly, then with more vigour. 'No. He couldn't. He wouldn't.' She searched her memory and a few minor incidents gnawed at her confidence.

Fergus went on. Quietly. Like a rumbling bulldozer. 'Don't tell me that; take a look at his pathology results. You need to ask why he would jeopardise his transplant.'

Ailee shook her head again but fear was like a hard rock in her chest. 'I do not, for a moment, believe this is true. But, if it were, what possible reason could he have?'

Fergus reached across to take her hand but she pulled her fingers out of his reach, unable to tolerate his sympathy, and the chasm, like a barren quarry between them, widened. Painfully. So many hard, rocky places in the road of this relationship.

Ailee went on without allowing Fergus to speak. 'He has no reason to do that.'

'He might.' Fergus pulled his coffee-cup closer and added sugar very slowly as if to give her time to calm down. 'I'm thinking guilt... or concern for you? Fears he can't cope with? Dread of rejection and that your sacrifice would all be for nothing? There are a hundred issues more mature people than William can't face. If he is too unwell for transplant, he doesn't have to admit any of those fears.'

Ailee planted her hands on the table. 'How long have you suspected this? Longer than today?'

His face didn't change. 'The tests were ordered last week, Ailee. What are you saying?'

She sniffed. 'You tell me. Is your professional judgement clouded by other issues?'

Fergus sat back as if she'd slapped him. 'You don't believe that.'

'No. I don't. I'm sorry.' Ailee covered her mouth with her hands and drew a deep breath before she spoke. 'This is all my fault for becoming involved with you and not concentrating on William. I need to think. I need to talk to William. Take me home, please Fergus.'

'As you wish.' He signalled for the check. 'William's problems need discussion and I'm sorry to upset you. It's a shock. But I am here for you, when you're ready.'

The drive home was accomplished in silence and Ailee opened her own door before Fergus could get out. She didn't think he was surprised.

'Thank you,' she said quietly.

'For what?'

'For agreeing to give me space.' She shut the car door, walked up the front path and didn't look back.

There wasn't a lot she could do this late at night and she wasn't going to think about Fergus. The hospital wouldn't thank her for waking up William in the ward bed and she couldn't share this with her mother.

Had William been drinking and consciously or subconsciously jeopardising his transplant chances? How had she missed that he was having second thoughts? Or maybe she did have suspicions and hadn't moved on to the possible conclusions. Fergus had. That was his job. It was hers too, but it was harder when it was family. She needed to give herself that break.

To add to that, of course Fergus was seeing possibilities she'd brushed aside because he'd already lost one woman in surgery and he was terrified to lose another.

She knew she'd been unfair to Fergus, but this was all part of the reason she hadn't wanted to get involved in the first place.

He'd clouded the issue and seduced her, though she'd been a very willing participant, and diluted her strength when she needed it most. She should have stayed away from him.

She'd been side-tracked but she'd change. She wouldn't make the same mistake again. She needed to talk to her brother and sort this out.

Chapter 19

Fergus

When Fergus arrived home it was ten o'clock and he doubted he'd sleep. Again. Luckily he didn't need much.

Ailee blamed herself for not noticing William's deviation earlier. Just so long as she didn't blame him if the decision to transplant was rescinded. He hoped Dr Harry would be back for that one.

Light was still angling from beneath Simone's bedroom door and he knocked gently in case she had fallen asleep reading.

'Hey, Dad.' His daughter sat up in bed and the smile she gave him eased some of the isolation he felt from the harsh words between him and Ailee.

'Hello, sweetheart. What are you doing awake?'

She glanced at the clock as if to say he was the late one. 'I wanted to wait for you to come home.'

'I'm home. Now go to sleep. It's school tomorrow.' Fergus crossed the room and pulled the curtains before coming back to sit on the edge of the bed.

'I know. Did you have a nice night with Ailee?' Simone was smirking at him as if she'd caught him out.

He appreciated her cleverness, but discussing Ailee with his daughter was the last thing on his wish list. 'What makes you think I was with Ailee?'

'Intuition.'

He raised his eyebrows and suppressed a smile. 'Really? What else does your intuition tell you?'

Simone tilted her head on one side and studied him. The mannerism belonged to her mother and he smiled.

'Things are not going smoothly,' his daughter pronounced.

'You have wonderful intuition, just like your mother had.' He tucked in her bedclothes. 'I love you but I'm not going to discuss this with you. Now, go to sleep.'

'Dad?'

This time he did smile. 'Yes, Simone.'

'Occasionally you have to take risks if something is important enough.' His world at this moment was full of irony, this time coming from Simone.

'Thank you, baby. I'll remember that.' He leant across and kissed his daughter on the brow. 'Goodnight.'

'Night, Dad.'

In the morning Simone was up before he left, which was unusual, and she dragged her fluffy slippers across the floor as she entered and shuffled across the room to slump into the chair next to him. 'I had a bad dream last night.'

Fergus put down his coffee and concentrated on his daughter. She looked pale.

'I'm sorry, sweetheart. You okay now?'

Simone shook her head and he saw that her eyes were red. She'd been crying.

'Not really,' she said softly.

Fergus stood up, pulled his daughter up against him and put his arms around her. She didn't pull away and his heart ached at how much she missed her mother in these growing years.

He dreaded the times in the future when their rapport might be lost. For the moment she trusted him again and he

accepted how much he needed that trust from his daughter. 'Do you want to tell me about it?'

She nodded her head, burrowing into his chest. He smoothed the fine hair back from her forehead. 'Take your time.'

Simone leant against him and then finally she mumbled into his shirt, 'Is Ailee sick?'

Fergus felt like groaning. 'Why do you ask?'

'Because in the dream she was sick like Mummy was. I was locked out of the room, looking through a window. You were sad and I was calling out to you, but you couldn't hear me.' Simone buried her nose back in his chest.

Fergus winced and rubbed her back. 'I will always hear you, baby.'

Simone looked up at him with tear-filled eyes. 'So Ailee isn't sick... is she?'

Now he was in a dilemma. 'No. Ailee isn't sick.' He felt his daughter relax against him with relief and he hugged her briefly. He wasn't lying but he wasn't being fair to his daughter either. 'Ailee's brother is sick.'

Simone stiffened against him. 'Can she catch it?'

'No.' He sighed. 'William is eighteen and has renal failure. You are probably one of the few girls in your school who would understand what that is and what it means to a previously healthy young person.'

Simone nodded and he drew a breath.

'Ailee is donating one of her kidneys to him in a week or two.'

His daughter froze and then pulled away to stare up into his face. 'But she might need it sometime herself.'

He tried to smile. 'Ailee is very healthy.'

Simone shook her head violently from side to side. 'Tell her she can't do it.'

He sighed and looked down at his daughter's pleading face. She was so young and fragile and had been through so much. 'I can't tell her that. It's Ailee's decision.'

Simone was still shaking her head. 'She could get sick. An infection or even a clot like Mummy! People die from operations. It's a big operation.'

'Ailee is not going to die.' His voice firm, sure, convincing her, convincing himself.

'Mummy wasn't supposed to die.'

And that was the crux of all of this. Fergus ached for the young girl who had watched her mother go into the hospital and never come out. 'I know, darling.' He hugged Simone to him but she pulled away.

'Why did you bring her here and make me like her if she's going to die?'

'I didn't make you like Ailee. You chose that yourself.' Firmly he said, 'And she's not going to die.'

Simone backed away out of his arms. 'Even if she doesn't die this time, one day she might get sick. She'll need her other kidney and it will be gone. Then she'll get sicker and sicker and die as well.'

Fergus stood there and watched his daughter back away from him. He tried to reason with her. 'Some people are born with one kidney and never have a problem. Perfectly healthy people who haven't donated can get sick kidneys suddenly. That is the same for everyone, Simone.'

Simone shook her head. 'You shouldn't have brought her here. I hate her and I hate you.' Simone spun on her heel and ran out of the room, and Fergus rubbed his face with his hand. Terrific.

Ailee would be saying 'I told you so'.

He wanted to knock his head against the wall. Or curse. Or hug Ailee to him.

Chapter 20

Ailee

On Tuesday morning Ailee arrived at the ward at the same time as the trolley bearing the breakfast trays.

Tossing in her bed, unable to sleep, she'd promised herself she'd stay focused on William and only William.

He had to have the transplant.

When she entered the ward her brother, face very pale, struggled to pull himself up in bed to eat.

'Good morning, William.' Ailee approached the bed and shifted his bedside table closer, unsure how to start the conversation.

'Ailee. You're early.' William studied his sister's face and something he saw there brought a look of wariness to his eyes. Ailee felt her stomach drop as he looked away.

He reached for the knife and buttered his toast intently. 'Have you come to steal my breakfast?' His attempt at lightening the mood fell flat and Ailee didn't help out.

'No. I've come to ask you some questions.'

'Like what?' There was a touch of bravado in the response and Ailee sighed.

'I think you've been drinking alcohol when you know it's bad for your condition. I thought you understood that.'

He glared at her. 'Who told you I was doing that?'

She leant on the breakfast table and tried to read his face. 'Your pathology results say so. Is there a problem, William?'

He shrugged. 'I've had a few beers with the boys. Sometimes more than a few. That's all.'

Fergus was right. Worst fears had been confirmed. Ailee shook her head. 'Your fluid limit has been consistently over and your biochem is through the roof.'

'Well, it won't matter if I get one of your healthy-as-Hades kidneys now, will it? Your kidney will fix everything.' The bitterness was clear this time.

Pain sliced into her without the need of a surgeon's knife. But all she could think to say was, 'They'll cancel the op if you prove yourself non-compliant.'

She thought she'd shock him with that but he just shrugged. 'What, no life-long corticosteroids and waiting for your ultimate sacrifice to stop working?'

Pain attacked, left her reeling like a victim in a knife frenzy. 'How long have you felt like this?' Ailee's hands came up to hold her stomach. She was a doctor, not just a sister, but distracted by Fergus she hadn't noticed he was in this state. She should have. Tears stung and her throat closed.

William glared at her. 'Since you came back. Go home, Ailee. I don't want to talk about it.'

This new William was a stranger, a hard, cruel, bitter stranger and she didn't know how to get through to him.

'We have to talk about it.' Ailee raised her hand towards his arm but he pulled away. 'What am I going to tell Mum?'

'Just leave it. Leave me. I'm not in the mood to talk about this.' His voice rose and a nurse looked across at them with concern on her face.

Nausea rose at the way her brother narrowed his eyes at her. She was doing no good here; she was making things worse.

She turned away and almost bumped into the ward sister who'd come across to see what William's raised voice was about.

'Everything okay?'

Ailee tried to smile. 'Fine. Sibling spat.' It was way more than that but her control was slipping. 'I'll be back later,' she said, and left the ward almost at a run.

Ailee went back to her office and sat in the chair with her head in her hands at the desk. Everything had been going so smoothly, or she'd thought it had. She'd been blind and stupid and distracted by the bright shininess of Fergus and falling in love when she should have been watchful and focused on her brother. Especially now.

First Fergus and her loss of control in Singapore, which she still couldn't believe, then his secondment slap in the middle of her workplace.

Put that with her inability to say no to him had her head spinning. She'd been diverted from seeing that William had gone into self-destruct mode. Dropped the ball.

She didn't know where to begin to make things right, except that she needed to stay away from Fergus and concentrate on her family.

Her mother would be devastated if they ran into problems at this late stage, but if she'd learned one thing these past weeks – it was not to delay telling the big truths. No matter how difficult, she needed to tell her mum. It would be more of a shock at the last minute.

And she started work in an hour.

How was she supposed to get through the day? This was the last place she felt like being... except rounds with Fergus would be even worse. She'd just have to work methodically through the obstacles and find solutions. Because there was too much at stake.

An hour later she was back on the ward and, thankfully, Fergus avoided any discussion with her during the round. He spoke most of the time with Rita and his registrar, often with the result that Rita had to ask Ailee to clarify some points, which Rita would then relay to Fergus.

Well, she had asked him for space, Ailee reminded herself as she stifled her own contrariness.

When they came to William, Ailee may as well not have been in the room. William refused to look at her and even Fergus noticed the strain between the siblings.

As they moved on, Ailee heard Fergus ask Rita to have the social worker see William today. And what worse things might the social worker find? Everything was going wrong.

Finally the round was over and Ailee had to hurry to meet her first appointment.

Fergus watched her go. He'd seen her crossed words with William this morning from Rita's office. He'd come in early, had planned on speaking to William before he saw his sister, but it had been too late.

The good news was that Ailee didn't know that he'd witnessed the exchange. She'd have hated that. The bad news was that he couldn't go after her and offer comfort because she wouldn't thank him.

He needed to step back and give her the space she'd asked for. He had a glimmer of an idea that could perhaps help and didn't involve him, but that was all he could do.

Maybe she was right. They would have been better to have left all this until after the transplant was completed.

Ailee's meeting was with a dark-haired, Samoan beauty; a mother planning to donate one of her kidneys to her son.

All of Teuila Tupuola's blood work had been completed and her scans and X-rays had been normal.

'It seems a lot of tests just to be able to give a kidney to my own son, Ailee.' Teuila looked at the already thick folder lying on Ailee's desk.

Tell me about it, Ailee thought, but knew they were necessary. 'I know, Teuila. It's to make sure you'll be well after donating your kidney. We'd look pretty silly if you only had one kidney, or only one working well, and we let you give it away.' Ailee held up the renal imaging studies and pointed. 'There are your two kidneys and this one shows the blood supply and structures in and around your kidneys, which are all normal.'

Teuila looked vaguely at the dark pictures and shrugged. 'If you say so.' She frowned. 'Because my son and I match blood groups, it's a good sign, isn't it?'

Ailee agreed. 'To be the same type is the best, but even a blood type your antibodies won't fight can be fine. People with O-type blood are still compatible to give but not receive from all the others, and AB-type blood, like yours and Fetu's, can receive from A, B, or O.'

'So how do they tell if Fetu's blood antibodies are going to fight with mine?'

'To cross-match, we take blood from you and Fetu, separate it down, and the laboratory incubates your lymphocytes with Fetu's serum. They look to see if Fetu has antibodies form to fight against your cells.' Ailee paused to allow Teuila time to understand that concept. 'Like unexpected milk lumps in your tea.

'Antibodies that are already formed, called preformed antibodies, can cause acute rejection after transplant. If antibodies already exist, the transplant can't go ahead. That's why some people are on waiting lists for years and others seem to have managed to jump the queue.'

Teuila nodded. 'I wondered about that.'

Ailee went on. 'It depends on the antibodies in the match as much, if not more, than how long you've been waiting.'

Teuila squinted at the results Ailee had facing her. 'So Fetu hasn't any preformed antibodies against my blood?'

Ailee smiled. 'None were found, so that is the best news.'

'Good then. When do we start talking about operation dates?' Teuila sat back and folded her plump arms across her ample breasts.

'It takes quite a while for all the tests to come back, and because transplanted kidneys don't always last for a long time, we make as much use of the failing kidneys as we can. It's usual to wait until just before someone like Fetu needs dialysis. Then we do the operation.'

Teuila drew her dark brows together. 'He might need another transplant in the future? How long will my kidney last?'

'It can vary, and we hope each kidney lasts a very long time. The majority of donor kidneys last between fifteen and thirty or more years if they are not rejected. Live donor kidneys, like yours, seem to last longer than those from someone unrelated who has died.'

Teuila nodded and Ailee went on. 'You must remember that the fifteen or thirty years we talk about means that someone like Fetu can have a normal life in that time. Even a shorter time than that makes a huge difference to a chronically ill person's quality of life.'

'You mention rejection. That seems to be the big worry.'

These were the more worrying aspects. 'And infection. Most renal experts believe the amount of acute rejection episodes Fetu has is a factor. That's why we keep a watchful eye on him for a long time.'

Teuila sighed. 'We seem to have been getting ready to do this for months and months. I just want it all to end.'

Ailee leant across and squeezed Teuila's hand. 'I know. I've been waiting to do the same for my brother for more than a year. It is a nerve-racking time. I even travelled overseas for a few months because my brother didn't need the operation at the time, but he's ready now.'

Ailee gritted her teeth as she said it. He'd better be. Teuila's eyes widened. 'When do you go in?'

Ailee thought of her last conversation with Fergus about William and stamped down her reservations. 'We're waiting for the final go-ahead from the surgeon, but it should be next week.'

When Ailee went back to see William that afternoon, she was dreading another confrontation.

But a different brother waited for her.

William smiled, somewhat sheepishly, but smiled nonetheless. 'I'm sorry, sis.'

Ailee felt the tears rush to her eyes and she stepped closer until William hugged her. She sank against him and hugged him back fiercely. 'I'm so sorry I didn't see how you were feeling.'

William brushed his own damp eyes. 'I'm sorry I was such a jerk.'

Ailee smiled and sniffed. 'You aren't a jerk but you scared me.' She tilted her head. 'What changed your mind?'

William half laughed. 'Who.'

It took Ailee a moment to get his meaning. 'Okay, then who changed your mind?'

'Lawrence.' William's face reddened. 'He practically kicked my butt he was so amazed at my stupidity.'

Ailee rocked back. Amazed. 'When did you meet Lawrence?'

'Mr McVicker introduced us.' William shook his head. 'And I thought I had it bad. Hell. Poor Lawrence, but don't tell him I said that.'

Ailee felt like hugging the absent patient. Bless Lawrence. 'I won't, but what did he say?'

'It was what he knew.' Judging by her brother's awed expression Lawrence obviously had made a big impression. 'He knew what I was thinking. How I felt. It was weird to hear it come from someone else's mouth. He said Mr McVicker wanted a commitment from me today or he would cancel the op.'

Ailee felt sick. She licked suddenly dry lips and put her hand over where her heart pounded faster. 'What did you do?'

William shook his head at the enormity of what could have happened. 'I got it. How stupid I'd been. How much I wanted to get on with my life. I asked to see Mr McVicker and said I would look after your kidney more carefully than anyone else in the world. He said I'd better or he'd be gunning for me.'

He grinned. 'It looks like we're going to Theatre next week, sis.'

On Wednesday, between ward rounds and transplant co-ordinator duties, Ailee was retested with another serum cross-match and tissue type to check that nothing had changed.

The new transplant co-ordinator would start on Monday and Ailee needed to ensure all her records and tasks were up to date. At least her workload meant she had little time to dwell on the disaster of her love life.

Any interaction with Fergus had dwindled to the barest minimum, and although he continued to treat everyone else with his usual warmth and care, Ailee was excluded from the circle with polite distance. It didn't escape her notice that this was exactly what she'd requested from Fergus.

On the Friday before the surgery, both she and William underwent the final psychological testing to ensure they were mentally ready for the operation. This time the results came back resoundingly affirmative.

After a subdued weekend spent lazing around at home with her family – and not one phone call from Fergus – Ailee was admitted on Monday afternoon as soon as William had his final dialysis. This admission there'd been no fluid overload on William's part, even though both he and Ailee had been on a clear fluid diet for the last twenty-four hours.

Ailee unpacked her hospital bag in the single room allocated to her. It was so weird to be the patient doing this stuff. She set up the bedside table for easy reach of things she imagined she might need when her movements would be severely restricted by the surgery.

As a quirk of her job, Ailee had quizzed Emma's husband, Peter, on any tips he might have for her in the post-operative period and he'd laughed quietly and said, 'Take the pain relief.'

The morning of the operation finally arrived and Ailee woke up on the ward. In a ward bed.

Dr Harry was back and would perform Ailee's surgery.

Fergus, on his last day at the hospital, would assist with William's transplant.

Ailee couldn't be happier with this surgical team. She could hear William's voice in the room next door as she slid her arms into her white hospital gown that threatened to expose everything to the world.

Her tummy rumbled more from nerves than the fact that she'd been fasting since midnight, and she imagined William felt the same. She slid a dressing gown over her theatre robe and poked her head into her brother's room.

'Morning, bro.' Ailee's nonchalance didn't quite come off but the new closeness with William excused that and they smiled at each other.

'Hungry?' Wiliam teased to hide his own nervousness, and they both looked up as the night sister came around with their charts to finalise the theatre requirements.

'I thought I'd find you in here, Ailee.' Greta had settled them to bed the previous night and had bullied Ailee into a sleeping tablet.

'I did sleep, Greta.' Ailee smiled at the nurse and she grinned back.

'Good. That's much better than you harassing me all night.' They both knew what she meant. 'A good sleep helps down the track.'

Greta smiled at William and then Ailee. 'I need some observations from both of you so pop back to bed because Dr Harry will be in soon and I have to do my duty before I go off.'

Ailee obediently went back to her room and climbed up into the bed. Her bedside table had been moved.

In her absence a basket of glorious Singapore orchids had arrived. The fragile blooms perfectly matched her fragile mood and the memories rushed back. Tears clouded her vision.

Chapter 21

Fergus

Fergus watched Ailee's hand stretch out to touch the velvet of a purple orchid, and the tightness in his chest prevented him from speaking. He cleared his throat and moved from the wall opposite the bed.

'Hello, Ailee.' It was all he could manage at that moment as the full impact of how close she was to going to theatre hit him in the heart — just like the day he'd first seen her – but even more now that he knew and loved her.

'The flowers are beautiful.' He could barely hear her voice for the rushing sound in his ears. He wanted to sweep her up into his arms and carry her away to safety, even though he knew the idea was ridiculous, because she was a strong and brave woman and didn't need saving. Just loving.

He cleared his throat again. 'I hope you don't mind but I needed to wish you well before you go in.'

'Thank you.' Ailee turned away and tried to brush the tears away without him seeing, but he came up in front of her and rested his hands on her shoulders.

Unable to help himself, he bent and kissed her lips and tasted the salt of her tears. 'Staying away has been the hardest thing, Ailee.'

Greta bustled into the room with her charts and Fergus stepped back as she spoke to the folders in her hand. 'So, all we need is…' She looked up and blinked when she saw Fergus was in the room. 'Mr McVicker?'

'I'm just leaving.' He looked at Ailee. 'I'll be in William's theatre. Good luck.'

Chapter 22

Ailee

Their eyes met for a final lingering look and for a moment Ailee thought he was going to lean in and kiss her again, but he left, almost in a rush – this wasn't easy for him she thought as she watched him go – knowing he carried her heart with him.

She wondered what they would have said to each other if there had been more time. But they were out of time. The orderly and trolley would be here soon to take her to theatre.

She lifted her chin. 'So what do you need, Greta?' Greta ticked the boxes on the pre-admission sheet. 'Just need to take your blood pressure and check your armband.'

Ailee nodded and lifted her arm.

An hour later Ailee lay on her back, slightly fuzzy from the pre-anaesthetic medication, on her way to the operating theatre. She'd always wondered what it would feel like to see the ceiling go past, like in the movies, so many times.

The air-conditioning vents streamed by, faceless voices came and went from her peripheral vision, and it seemed to take forever to arrive at the swinging plastic doors of the operating theatres.

A figure clad in a scrub suit took her hand and checked her armband. 'Hello. Can you tell me your name and what operation you are having today?' Ailee had heard it all so many times and now it was her turn.

After the first check they passed through into the anaesthetic room and Andrew was all bouncy good humour.

'So, Ailee—' he said as he patted her wrist and squared up to impale her vein with an incredibly large cannula '—bet you never thought you'd see me from this angle.'

'If you didn't have a mask on, I'd be able to see up your nose,' she bantered back, but the nerves were starting to squirm inside at what lay ahead and some of it must have shown in her eyes.

Andrew dropped his humour and patted her shoulder. 'You'll be fine, my friend. We need your sort around here. I'll take good care of you.'

'I know you will. Just make sure your colleague next door takes good care of William, too.'

'Done. Now, off you go to sleep.'

And that was the last Ailee heard.

Chapter 23

Fergus

Fergus couldn't stay away as he waited for his own operation to start. He hovered around the theatre doors, not able to cope with the viewing-room window, and went over in his mind what would be happening inside.

Ailee's kidney would be removed first and the operation would take about an hour. His love lay in the theatre next door and William would come into this theatre when Ailee's kidney was ready. The scrub room lay between the two theatres.

Fergus had checked and Dr Harry had chosen to use the open-excision method he'd used for thirty years. Fergus admitted to less chance of injury to the donor organ than the keyhole method of excision if the surgeon wasn't as used to laparoscopic nephrectomy. He just wished Ailee hadn't had to suffer the extra recovery time, pain, and movement restriction from the large excision.

Although William's operation would take twice as long as Ailee's, Ailee would be the one with the extended recovery time and greater shock to the system because she'd previously been well. William would start to feel better almost immediately.

But Fergus had no say, either in her choice of surgeon or anything to do with her life. She'd told him that.

An hour passed. 'What are you doing out here?' Dr Harry said as he slipped out of his sterile gown to have a small break before he had to re-scrub to assist Fergus with William's operation.

'Waiting for a friend. Is she out yet?'

The older surgeon smiled. 'I thought you might be. She's fine. And the young fellow will come along well, too.' He looked at Fergus from under his brows. 'She's just going through to Recovery now and isn't really awake. Go on through and see her.'

Fergus had been debating, but Dr Harry was on a mission now. 'We can afford a few minutes before we start on young William. There has to be some bonus for all the extra hours we work.' Dr Harry's bushy eyebrows bounced up and down. 'So that's why you didn't want to do this one, eh?'

'As you say.' Fergus didn't enlarge on the subject and the older man didn't pursue it.

They entered the recovery area and Fergus picked out Ailee at twenty paces. She was asleep. Her face pale and the intravenous line running a blood transfusion so she must have lost a bit. Or a lot.

She was so pale. He sucked in his breath in shock.

Dr Harry heard the noise. 'She had a little bleeder, but we got it in the end.' He looked at Fergus and almost chuckled. 'She probably didn't need the blood but it saved her feeling tired for the next month, so don't look at me like that.'

This was a common enough complication for patients, but not for Fergus, and not for Ailee. There was no escaping his need for this woman, and while he'd loved and mourned his first wife this was for now and the future, and his future revolved around this woman.

There were obstacles before them, but as he looked down at her, unconscious and moaning gently in her sleep, he vowed to himself he would have and hold his Ailee.

It might take time but Simone would get used to the idea.

He moved across and lifted Ailee's hand to his cheek. She felt cold and he warmed her fingers between his hands before tucking them back under the covers.

He lifted his head. He had a job to do.

As Fergus cleaned his nails with the brush in the scrub room, he averted his eyes from the container where Ailee's kidney waited to be transplanted.

Fergus entered the theatre and strode to the table. William lay anaesthetised, his abdomen exposed. The scrub sister handed Fergus the bowl and sponge forceps so he could prep.

He drew a deep breath. Renowned for his perfectionism, this would be his most meticulous transplant yet.

'Now, that's a beautiful kidney,' Dr Harry said nonchalantly.

'It's the most beautiful kidney in the world,' Fergus stated, and then he cleared his mind of the external distractions and set about placing Ailee's kidney in William's pelvis.

The donor kidney was seated near William's bladder so that the ureter could be easily connected through an incision in the lower part of his body. William's old kidneys would not be removed. It took hours.

Chapter 24

Ailee

When Ailee surfaced slowly through the anaesthetic mist, she realised she had returned to her bed on the ward. Gingerly she turned her head and it seemed there were bright splotches around every wall. That was funny — she hadn't noticed those that morning.

The next time she woke she realised the splotches were arrangements of flowers — baskets and baskets of orchids and bougainvillea. She didn't need anyone to tell her who'd sent them.

Her throat hurt and she ran her roughened tongue over dry lips.

'Have some ice,' a deep voice said, and she opened her mouth for the chip of ice without worrying why Fergus was there. She smiled dreamily.

Of course he was.

She savoured the feeling as ice disintegrated the dryness of fur on her tongue.

The intravenous lines in her arm caught on the sheet and a large hand came across and gently disentangled them for her. She turned her head slowly and found him sitting in the chair beside her bed.

'Hello, sleepyhead. How is your pain?'

'Not too bad if I don't move,' she croaked.

'You have to move a bit. Don't forget your "dope-on-a-rope".' He slid the controls of her patient-controlled analgesia into her hand. 'Press your button for drugs when you have pain. It works quickly and it won't let you overdose.'

'Yes, Doctor.' She was too tired to fight against how good it was to see him.

'Cheeky already.'

'Mmm-hmmm,' she murmured, and fell asleep again.

The next time she woke up, her mother was sitting at her bedside and she wondered if she'd dreamed up Fergus in that same chair. Her mother offered her some ice. 'How are you, darling?'

'Fine, Mum.' She shifted her head and the pain in her flank reminded her to be careful. She felt the control in her hand and gave herself a click of pain relief. She had to move. When the pain receded, she sighed and smiled at her mother. 'How's William?'

'He's doing well up in High Dependency. His new kidney is working already.'

'That's great.' She stretched out her arm gingerly and she couldn't believe how that simple movement could set off so many pain receptors in her side. Her mother picked up the cup of ice and handed it to her and she took another piece. Heavenly.

Chapter 25

Fergus

Three days after Ailee and William's operations, Fergus could wait no longer.

'Simone, we need to talk.'

Fergus hoped she was ready to talk about Ailee now without becoming upset. His daughter had been avoiding him and every time he broached the subject she drifted away, but he was wearing her down. He ached for her pain but he needed her to know that he hadn't deliberately set out to hurt her.

'I'm listening.' Simone didn't meet his eyes but at least she'd sat down this time.

Fergus sat next to her and took her hand in his. 'I'm sorry I hurt you with my friendship with Ailee, but three days ago Ailee had her operation and she's getting better now.'

He watched the words sink in and to his relief she didn't pull away or run screaming from the room.

'The thing is, sweetheart, I've grown to love Ailee and I want to include her in our lives.'

Simone sighed. 'I know, Dad. I guess I saw it the first day you brought her home. I think I could love her, too. And I'm sorry I said all those things about hating you both, but it is pretty scary thinking that what happened to Mummy could happen to Ailee.' Her eyes met his. 'I don't ever want to be that sad again.'

Fergus squeezed her hand. 'Neither do I, baby, but I think we could be really happy with Ailee in our lives.'

Fergus caught his daughter's chin gently and looked into the eyes so similar to his own. 'And who was the person who told me we all have to take risks if something is important enough?'

Simone rolled her eyes. 'Me.'

He slipped his arm around her shoulders and hugged her. 'I love you, Simone, and I always will. And we will be a family, hopefully with Ailee as a part of it.'

'I hope so, too.'

He wondered how far he could stretch their new friendship. 'I'm going in to visit her today... Would you like to come?'

To his intense relief Simone nodded.

Chapter 26

Ailee

Ailee turned her head and her mouth tilted when she saw Fergus, then her eyes widened when she saw who was standing beside him at the door.

'Simone came in slowly and looked reassured to see Ailee sitting up in a chair beside the bed. 'Can I speak to Ailee on her own, Dad?'

Fergus looked across and raised his eyebrows. 'I guess so, if it's fine with Ailee.'

Ailee nodded. 'Sure.'

'How are you?' Simone crept close but was careful not to bump the chair.

Ailee patted the seat next to her and waited while Simone sat down. 'I'm getting better every day.'

Simone studied her fingers before looking up. 'How come you weren't scared to give away your kidney?'

'You didn't see me on the morning of the operation.' Ailee spread her hands to measure the size. 'I had butterflies bigger than bats in my tummy.'

'Yes.' Simone smiled at the thought. 'But how come you still gave it away?'

Ailee tilted her head. 'I think what you are asking is why I did something you think is a little dangerous when I didn't have to... am I right?'

Simone nodded.

'When my brother first became unwell, my mother thought just like you. She didn't want to risk me getting sick, too, and she was frightened something would go wrong. Say I didn't give my kidney to my brother...' Ailee tilted her head. 'Imagine if William became really sick and died and I never got sick and lived to be an old lady with two kidneys.'

She looked into Simone's eyes. 'I think I'd be pretty sad and selfish at the end. I'd know I hadn't dared to give up something I didn't need just in case something went wrong, when I could have easily saved my brother's life.'

Simone raised her beautifully arched eyebrows not unlike her father's. 'I don't think it was easy, what you did.'

Ailee smiled. 'Maybe not, but I have spent a lot of time around sick people – especially those with end-stage renal disease – and they have a challenging life with a lot of things taken away from them. From where they're sitting, I bet what I did looks easy.'

Simone nodded, semi-converted but not convinced. 'What if you get kidney disease later in life and need a kidney?'

'The chance of that is smaller than a lot of things. What if I get run over by a bus or travelled to another country and had an accident?' Ailee gave a tiny shrug. 'Should I stay home safely just in case? Should you not go skiing because it's dangerous and certainly not go to New Zealand because it's a long way from home?'

'I'm sorry I got scared,' Simone said in a small voice.

Ailee held open her arms and Simone crept closer to lean gently against her. 'I'm sorry I scared you, but it was very nice of you to care what happened to me.' She stroked Simone's hair. 'Do you want to know a secret?'

Simone nodded and Ailee went on in a whisper. 'There was one thing I was scared of. I wouldn't let myself fall in love with your father in case something went wrong.'

Simone leant back so she could see Ailee's face. 'And now that you are getting better?'

Ailee raised her eyes to the man standing at the door, trying not to eavesdrop. 'As soon as I'm well, I'm going to chase him as hard as I can.'

'Okay,' Simone whispered back.

Ailee looked up and her mother was standing beside Fergus at the door.

'Hi, Mum, come in.' Ailee smiled at Simone.

Helen and Fergus came to stand beside the chairs. 'This is Simone, Fergus's daughter. Simone, my mum.'

Helen smiled. 'Hello, Simone. It's lovely to meet you.' Helen raised her eyebrows at her daughter, as if to say, *Why didn't you tell me?*

Ailee mouthed, *Later.* Her mother smiled.

Helen looked at Simone. 'Would you like to come and meet Ailee's brother, William?'

Simone nodded and stood up. She smiled at Ailee. 'Ailee wants to talk to Dad anyway.'

'Does she now?' said Helen, and both were grinning conspiratorially as they left.

Fergus sat down beside her and took her hand in his. 'That didn't seem to go too badly from where I was standing.'

'How did you convince Simone to visit?'

He shrugged ruefully. 'She seemed ready. I found her looking up live donor websites on the internet yesterday. I think she'll be fine. I know she'll be happier when you're safely home. As will I!'

Ailee smiled and squeezed the larger hand in hers. 'I understand.'

He looked at her and smiled. 'I don't think you do.'

'I think Simone is very brave and wonderful, like her father.'

'I haven't started to be brave yet,' he said cryptically. 'Now, how are you today?'

She looked down at their entwined fingers and savoured the feeling. Fergus had been a little more open with his affection every day since her operation, and she was happy to let it all progress slowly while she recuperated. The warmth of expectation had been growing since that first morning when he had been there when she'd woken up.

'I'm better every day, Fergus.' Fergus. Yep. She loved saying his name.

'Keep going.' His eyes were warm. 'How about you come home to my house to recuperate instead of your mother's?'

Ailee wrinkled her brow. 'Are you going to take up nursing, Mr McVicker?'

Now they were heated. 'Only one patient. And I was thinking full-time care.' He paused. Said softly, 'Forever.'

Ailee looked up at the serious tone of his voice.

He shook his head. 'You still don't get it. 'Do you realise how much I love you and have loved you since the first time I saw you?'

She kept her mouth shut, maybe she was beginning to realise. Especially with the way he was looking at her now. 'I knew you fancied me,' she teased.

He waggled his brows at her. 'That, too, but I was thinking "ever after" when you woke beside me on the plane that first morning.'

Ailee's eyes widened. 'That can't be true.'

His lips twitched. 'I'm afraid so. Why do you think I was so mean to you when you arrived on the ward? You broke my heart when you left me in Singapore.'

She looked him up and down. 'You look pretty hale and hearty for someone with a broken heart.'

He squeezed her hand back. 'I know you won't get away this time. I can relax!'

Despite the banter, she realised he'd given up on waiting and she couldn't ask him to wait any longer. He'd been patient enough. He smiled at her crookedly and Ailee felt the tears prickle her eyes. He was her soulmate. The one she'd waited for.

For a moment, her decisive man looked uncertain. So unlike him. 'I want to do this properly. I should wait for you to be strong and for the setting to be somewhere romantic.' He glanced at the floor. 'But I'm not waiting.' Warned her. 'I'm going to kneel.'

Ailee bit her lip and swallowed the lump in her throat. 'Don't you dare.'

Ignoring that, Fergus dropped to one knee beside the chair. His expression grew serious, intent as he took her hand. Raised his gaze to hers. 'Darling, darling Ailee. Would you please do me the very great honour of becoming my wife?'

Ailee reached across, careful of her wound, and kissed his lips. 'I would be privileged, Fergus. Thank you. Now, get up quickly before someone sees you.' She glanced furtively at the empty doorway.

Fergus smiled now. Joyfull. Teasing. Amused. 'No, I think I'll ring the nurse's call button and get Rita in here to see what you've brought me to.'

Ailee tugged on his hand. 'Fergus. Get up. And don't make me laugh. It hurts.'

He climbed to his feet and bent to kiss her. 'The last thing I want to do is hurt you. In fact, I'm going to spend the next fifty years looking after you.'

Ailee smiled unsteadily at the man she'd waited so long to find and loved with all her heart. 'And I'll look after you, my love.'

They held a makeshift engagement party on the ward with lemonade and ice-cubes and paper cups, Rita found a balloon from somewhere and all the nurses toasted them. Simone looked down at William in his wheelchair, as they watched the two love birds hold hands, and she touched William's shoulder. 'That was quick,' Simone said. 'I've always wanted a brother.'

Chapter 27

Fergus

The wedding was held in the gardens of Fergus's home with red and gold lanterns strewn among the trees. The exotic mix of Singapore orchids and splashes of vivid ruby from branches of bougainvillea highlighted the scarlet cheongsam worn by the young bridesmaid as she stepped to the head of the aisle between the people-filled rows of white chairs.

The Wedding March began.

Head high and smiling, Simone slowly paced down the carpet stretched in a ribbon of red across the grass that led to the roofless chapel Fergus had created for his bride.

For the last month he'd watched his daughter and Ailee do all the feminine things Simone should have been doing for the last few years. Clothes shopping and hairdresser visits. Hilarious dancing lessons so Simone and William could dance with the bride and groom at the reception. Redecorating her bedroom and interfering in the refurbishment of what would now be Fergus and Ailee's room.

Fergus watched with pride as his daughter swayed sedately up the aisle and took her place beside him as they waited for the bride.

'You look beautiful,' Fergus said, as Simone arrived.

'Wait until you see Ailee,' Simone whispered.

'I can't,' Fergus whispered back.

An indrawn gasp of delight from those assembled heralded the bride's arrival.

His gaze fastened on the vision of his bride-to-be as she stood, paused and looked his way. Her mouth tilted in that gorgeous smile he adored, her eyes sparkled and shone with so much love he felt the pain in his throat as so many emotions rose in his chest.

The music swelled.

Fergus had waited for this day for three months. Accompanied by a new and vibrant William, Ailee held his gaze from the end of the carpet.

She'd chosen to dress simply in a pure white, high- collared sheath that accentuated her height and slimness, and a tiny veil that Fergus ached to lift. Graceful, like a dancer she swayed towards him, tightening his already rigid chest and filling his soul with homecoming.

When Ailee stopped at the flower-strewn altar, William transferred her fingers from his arm to Fergus's.

She looked at him, the man she loved, and exhilaration expanded in Fergus's chest. He wanted to sweep her up in his arms and spin her around. Finally this moment had arrived and he couldn't help but look at the minister to get on with it.

'Dearly beloved... ' The minister hurried into speech and Fergus held Ailee's gaze as the words washed over them. 'I love you,' he whispered, and squeezed her hand.

'I love you, too,' she said, and he could see the shine of happy tears in her eyes. He loved her so much he hoped he could speak the vows through the tightness in his throat.

But when the time came, both their promises carried clearly across the garden.

Fergus gazed into Ailee's eyes, hoping she knew how proud he was to stand beside her. In this moment and forever.

When the service was complete, Fergus lifted the tiny veil and her face was there before him. They smiled at each other and then he bent and rested his lips against hers to taste the sweetness to come. He kissed his bride, finally sure that everything would turn out right.

Ailee and Fergus turned to the congregation and Fergus tucked his wife's hand firmly into his arm, leaving no one in any doubt that he meant to keep Ailee close by his side.

The minister's voice boomed. 'It is my pleasure to introduce Mr Fergus and Dr Ailee McVicker.' The applause washed over the happy couple as they walked back up the carpet.

Within minutes guests milled and spilled out into the garden and the sun shone down on everyone.

Ailee's mother sniffed happily into a handkerchief lent to her by Dr Harry's wife.

William and Simone came up to congratulate them and there was a twinkle of mischief in Ailee's brother's eyes.

'Hey, bro,' he said, with a smile to Fergus. 'I'll take great care of her kidney if you take good care of the rest of her.'

Fergus laughed. 'I'll be spending my life doing that,' he said, as squeezed the precious fingers of the woman he loved.

About the Author

Fiona McArthur has written more than fifty books and shares her medical knowledge and her love of working with women, families and emergency services in her stories.

In her compassionate, pacy fiction, her love of the travel and the Australian landscape meshes beautifully with warm, funny, multigenerational characters as she highlights challenges for rural and remote families, overseas adventures, big city hospitals and the strength shared between women.

There will be romance. Fiona means to make that gorgeous heroic man earn the right to win his beautiful and strong-willed heroine's heart because absolutely, happy endings are a must.

Fiona is the author of the non-fiction book *Aussie Midwives,* and lives on a farm with her husband in northern New South Wales. She was awarded the NSW Excellence in Midwifery Award in 2015. The NZ Koru Award in 2019 for short romantic fiction and the Australian RUBY Award for Contemporary Romantic Fiction 2020.